LIBRARIAN

LIBRARIAN

Peter Abbot

Rock's Mills Press

Oakville, Ontario

PUBLISHED BY

Rock's Mills Press

This is a work of fiction. No reference is intended to actual persons, places, or events.

Library and Archives Canada Cataloguing in Publication data is available from the publisher. Email us at customer.service@rocksmillspress.com or visit us online at www.rocksmillspress.com.

Cover illustration: Sharon Trottier
Cover background image: Freeimages.co.uk

ISBN-13: 978-1-77244-017-1

LIBRARIAN

I

11 December 2021

Last man on earth—I'm beginning to fantasize that. The last human survivor! Seems very unlikely, in a world inhabited by so many millions of people in so many cities, so many countries. But in this silence—who knows? Actually, I think it's the silence, and my deepening sense of isolation, that are encouraging me to think I may be alone, completely alone. — But how will I find out for sure, now that radio and TV and newspapers and the Internet and of course the social media have all gone? So, don't even think about it! If I *am* the last, there's nobody out there to care! Keep active, exercise—think and write. No returned books to re-shelve now—or very few, the final few. However, I always did find pleasure and some company, or illusion of company, in books—and in my own writing, those unpublished poems and short stories piled up in my closet at home! So now here I am taking refuge again in the comfort of words? Beloved words! Of course nobody will read the ones I write now, almost certainly they won't. So who am I writing them for? Myself, I guess. My other self. The urge to communicate remains, remains to the end?—even if only with oneself.

The silence, the silence, the silence. More than the darkness at night, and the gloom during the day, this long unbroken silence disturbs and distresses me. Especially since Thumper died, two days ago—my dearest companion, my loving

Thumper. Not that he was ever noisy—'Thumper' turned out to be an inappropriate name for him, inherited from his father, Old Thumper. —His nibblings and murmurings and rustlings were my benison. I loved him deeply—his gentle fragility, his pure white coat and big shiny round black eyes and twitching pink nose—most of all, his charming kind unassuming personality. I buried him yesterday afternoon next to Mum—who also loved him, she called him 'Peter's Rabbit' sometimes, a humorous reference to me and to Beatrix Potter's *Tale of Peter Rabbit*, which she had often read to me when I was a small boy.

So— How did I get to be here, where I'm sitting, in this University Library? All on my own, surrounded, outside the University Librarian's Office, by shelves and shelves and shelves of books, books, many thousands of books—and in the big reading rooms, by table after table laden with blank-screened computers. Dad—it was Dad's idea. That's how it began. I used to hear him and Mum talking in bed late at night—they didn't realize that I could hear them of course, and I never told them. —It was through the heating vents—my bedroom was beside theirs, and it was only when the furnace got going in winter— we had real winters then, icy snowy cold ones—that I couldn't hear almost every word they said to each other. They slept in separate beds, and most nights they would talk for a while before going to sleep, about what had happened to each of them during the day, or about what they would be doing the next day, or about something troubling them. Yes, and often that was *me*, they always worried about me. I remember how that time, when I was sixteen, they were worried that I was still being bullied—and I was, but they decided they couldn't do anything about it without making me even more unpopular, even more of a target, and maybe they were right. "And his grades are weak and getting worse, he won't make university entrance, will he?" Mum asked, deferring to Dad about academic matters as always—after all, he was the University Librarian, and she was a mere social worker. "No, he won't, the way he's going. And he doesn't seem to care. However much I talk to him, you know how often, he just—well, we spoilt him, especially before we adopted Fiona, in those years when he was still the apple of your eye." "Oh, Barry, now don't do that blaming me again." "No, I'm not blaming you, just trying to understand *him*, why he is as he is—doesn't enjoy sport and says he's no good at it, so he refuses to do it, and why? it's not as if he's obese—and yet he doesn't make any effort with his academic studies either—he certainly doesn't take after me and my family, or you and your family either. What *is* he interested in?" "I think it's mainly because of Fiona—I've been thinking that lately. When we adopted her, maybe he thought that meant we didn't love him any more, whatever we *said*, and however much we tried to show him we do love him—I've tried so hard to compensate, you know that, Barry, but it just doesn't seem to change anything with him." "Yes, yes, I know—we've said all of this before, often enough, and we both have a lot of other things on our minds, and we get home every evening exhausted—and there's nothing we can do now, is there? He's just—evasive. You can't get a real answer out of him. Thank goodness Fiona's different." "Well, if you—" "'—would take more interest in him'—please let's not get into that again, Julie. You know I do my best, you know how busy I am, how many problems there are these days—just getting minimal funding is harder than ever, with all the damn cutbacks. But I do have an idea, and if it works it might do the trick and also satisfy all of us, temporarily anyway. You remember how he enjoyed going on that Library tour and being in my Office with me that week last term? Well, he could work in the Library—mainly re-shelving books, we always need more people for that—he wouldn't make much money, it would be only a part-time summer position—but it would be a *job* and maybe it would be stimulating, give him some pride, a focus in life." Thanks, Dad—it did! In fact, after that summer, and continuing failure at high school during the next year—by then they were saying I was autistic or whatever, or was it ADHD, those psychiatrists they sent me to—because I wouldn't 'co-operate', meaning I wouldn't converse nicely and politely with them, answer all their stupid questions, and one of them, the old bald one, always wanted to test my 'total recall', as if he couldn't believe I had it—so I dropped out, I just refused to go, and by the time I turned eighteen I was employed full-time at the Library. Mum wasn't happy about that, but she was mainly worried about Fiona's diabetes by then—of course she had wanted me to stay on at high school, they both did, and go to university, and get a degree, and have a career—but Dad said "The job's only temporary anyway" so she stopped talking about it, to him or me. She had also been worried that my employment in the Library was somehow illegitimate, because I was the Librarian's son. "Oh, don't worry about that" Dad told her. "Nobody will be bothered, or even notice probably. As University Librarian, I do have a few prerogatives! It's only a menial job anyway, what he'll be doing. And I'll be able to keep an eye on him." I remember looking up "menial" in my dictionary next morning, to check that I knew its meaning accurately, and its etymology.

I've left out a few facts, I guess one always does—impossible to describe anything with total accuracy and completeness. And maybe I've put together in one conversation what I remember from several of my parents' conversations at the time. But that's basically how it happened, why and how I have worked quietly and mostly happily here for so many years, more than twenty actually! amongst my beloved books, and living quietly at home. Dad, he did it. And our house is just over the road, almost opposite the main entrance to the University—students were always throwing stuff on our lawn, condoms and empty bottles mainly, and pissing and vomiting on it late at night after getting drunk at parties—but Dad always said it was a stroke of luck he had been able to rent and then buy a house so conveniently close to the Campus when he and Mum had just arrived from Scotland, two-and-a-half years before I was born—Dad was actually English by birth, he grew up in Leicester, but he met Mum in Edinburgh when he started working in the Scottish National Library. And it was lucky for me too! What would have happened to me if I couldn't be here, in this Library? Even now, in the silence— But maybe it's not total silence, the books sort of talk to me, sometimes, and I sort of talk to them—we keep each other company. And now I *live* here too, in the Library, it's my home—now that Mum and Dad are dead, and Thumper too, soon after Mum. After Thumper was gone, I went back to our house only a few times, to get clothes and food, and now I have enough here that I brought over, cans and cans of veggies and meat and soup and fruit and juice, and plastic bottles of water—enough food and drink to last for at least a month! so I don't need to go to our house again for a while, or even go outside at all—but I do go outside sometimes, to look at the Campus, and especially at the big old maple tree that stands halfway between the Library and our house—I've always loved it—but it has no leaves at all now and I'm afraid it's dead, because of yet another very hot dry summer this year, the hottest one so far, and no rain— Just three years ago, in the Fall, it had some bright red foliage, and it was still quite shady and beautiful. And the grass everywhere is dead too, dry and brown. One night I woke up, feeling a bit cold— the Library's heating has stopped now—so I brought some blankets over from our house—but still it's warm for the time of year, and no sign of snow again so far! Maybe it'll be another non-winter winter—the weather's been crazy for years. No lights too, anywhere, of course—the Hydro stopped completely two nights ago, just suddenly stopped and all the lights went out —so now I lie in the dark, on the couch in Dad's Office, under a blanket, and just think about everything and anything, and try to remember happy experiences, especially the ones with Elise, and Thumper, and Mum and Dad, until I fall asleep.

What has happened to Fiona, I wonder? And Eric her husband and their two adopted children—they live in Washington, D.C.—Eric's a diplomat. They all came to see Dad in hospital after his first heart attack, and Fiona came on her own for his funeral a month later, and that was the last time I saw her. When she went back to Washington, she said she would write or telephone or e-mail, but she didn't, or maybe she couldn't if she left it too late. I liked the two kids, Danielle and Francois, black kids adopted as orphaned babies after the earthquake in Haiti—they were very gentle with Thumper, just enjoyed petting and stroking him, he loved that! AIMD, this virus or whatever it is, it had already started, before Dad got sick, but it wasn't here yet, or even in Europe, it was still mainly in Africa and South America, and China and India, and they didn't know what it was and they still don't—but Dad, he told Mum The End was coming, after he read articles in the newspapers and magazines about AIMD, and it was on the TV news a whole lot—at that time they would say how fast it was spreading, and they were always asking each other where would it appear next? and estimating how many millions of people it had already killed—there was no way to control it, because of refugees and people traveling from one country to another, spreading the infection— As I said, they stopped all that traveling eventually, and tried to prevent anyone coming to Canada or leaving—but it was too late by then, it was a pandemic here too. And there are no new antibiotics to try to control it—the old ones are ineffective through long over-use, that's what they said. Panic was spreading everywhere. Dad told Mum he had had a dream one night, a Voice told him to get ready, we all must get ready, get ready, get ready—and Mum said "Surely not, it's your imagination, Barry, 'ready' to do what?"—but then he got angry and started shouting "All right, don't believe me if you don't want to—that's what they said to Noah too, didn't they, until the Flood came," and she laughed and said "Oh, *Barry!*"and then he calmed down after she said he would wake me up with his shouting—but before he stopped he said that the Voice told him there would be seven months of famine and disasters, and then The End would come for the whole world. After that night, he went out in his car every afternoon and came back with big cardboard boxes full of cans and bottles and packets, and stored them in the basement. I could see Mum was worried about him, especially when she was home and he would drive off in a hurry—this was all before he had his first heart attack—she told me she wondered if one day he might not get home, or would crash the car. He wasn't University Librarian any more by then, he had retired and the new one had taken his job—the young one from New York, Dr Goode, who filled the Library with computers, so the students didn't read books any more, but sat around with their laptops and got all their information and critical opinions by Googling—Dad said, when he heard about all of that, it made him sick, and I guess it did—and he just went on getting worse and worse. "Your Father is declining, we have to try to help him" Mum said to me. "I can't talk to him about most things now, he gets so angry, and just raves, you've heard him—and sometimes he doesn't even know who I am. The doctor said it's dementia—Alzheimer's. Try to talk to him, darling? Just quietly and gently." But he also didn't know who *I* am, his own son, and one day he shouted "I do not approve of what you are doing to the Library, Dr Goode, distracting the students from reading books, encouraging them to sit around and chatter and go on Facebook and Twitter, and spend their time and energy putting stupid personal information on blogs, and reading each other's blogs—the Library is meant to be a place for books and journals and silent study and disseminating knowledge, not chattering and throwing parties and taking drugs, it's not meant to be a social centre! You are destroying wisdom, Dr Goode" and I held his hands, they were shaking, and I looked into his angry frightened eyes and just said calmly "I am so sorry you disapprove of the changes I have initiated, Sir, but there's nothing you can do now, is there, nothing at all, why not just relax? — You see, I have the power to do exactly what I like in the Library because I am the one in charge, I am the University Librarian" and I am.

But is this all a dream? —A nightmare? Yet how could that be? I'm sitting at Dad's desk in the University Librarian's Office, right here, right now, and I'm writing these words in this notebook— But could I be in a sort of "alternative reality," like in those SF books I used to read when I was a teenager? But then— No, surely not— No, because then I'm crazy—and I'm not. So go on writing, go on writing— Look, all these words, phrases, clauses, sentences that I'm writing in this notebook, right here—they make sense, don't they? So stop this. Stop! I am I, I am real, I am in the real world, or what's left of it. I am real in the real world.

When Mum got ill, I didn't know what to do. She was in bed, moaning and crying, and she wouldn't eat anything and I knew she was in pain, so I gave her Tylenols—and I got into the bed with her to make her calm and warm, and put Thumper on her stomach because she liked stroking him. After a while, she fell asleep and I walked across to the University Hospital to try to find a doctor, or a nurse, or anyone who could help—but there was nobody, it was empty, and silent, like the street outside—only there were bodies of patients in their beds, children, when I looked into one ward—and there was a strange unpleasant smell, like a mixture of disinfectant and vomit—so I went back home. Mum was still asleep, but she was moaning, and had bad diarrhea—the mess and smell were awful, it took me a while to clear it all up—I tried to call her doctor but there was only silence on the line, which was what I expected of course, and I knew already you couldn't e-mail, the Internet is dead and gone. Of course this was before I moved into the Library—I mean, to *live* here—I had been looking after her and feeding her ever since she stayed in bed after Dad's funeral—it was only two weeks since then, but the silence had started before—there was hardly any movement, hardly anyone to be seen in the neighborhood or on the campus, and no buses, and hardly any cars, and now there seems to be no movement out there at all—and she didn't say anything, she just stopped talking and closed her eyes. At Dad's funeral, in the United Church in Westgreen, there had been only the Minister, and Mum and Fiona and me—Fiona had to get a special permit to be allowed to cross the border from Buffalo into Ontario—I guess nobody else knew he had died, there were no newspapers by then, and I didn't think to try to call and tell people. —But even if his friends and ex-colleagues had known, any who were still here, probably they would have stayed away because everyone was terrified of getting AIMD—for several months by then, nobody would shake hands or hug, and they would turn their heads away from each other—it was killing more and more people here in Canada as well as in so many other countries, I heard the Minister say that to Mum. I wonder if she died from AIMD, Mum—her skin seemed to be turning brown—and if the Minister has died from it too—I tried to call her when I got back from the Hospital and saw that Mum was dying, but as I said there was just silence on the line. So I sat on the bed, beside her, and held her hand, and Thumper sat on her stomach—she was hardly breathing, and after a while she just sighed and died. I buried her in the yard, near the edge of the ravine, in her best dress, the pale blue one. Dad was cremated, he had arranged that long before, and after he died the undertakers collected his body from the Hospital, and then they wheeled it into the

Church—the Minister was new, she didn't know Dad, and in her eulogy she hardly mentioned him, just repeated over and over again that Death is not Death, it's only a door opening into the everlasting joy of our new life with Jesus in Heaven—and after the service the two men wheeled Dad away in a shiny black coffin. I thought we would go to the Cremation, but Mum said no, she couldn't bear that, so we didn't—she leaned on me all the way to the car, trembling and crying softly. When I buried her, the soil was quite hard, it's clay, and I got very tired with all the digging and shoveling—I had recited the Lord's Prayer and what I could remember of Psalm 23 while she was lying on her bed, before I carried her out into the yard, I knew she'd want that. When I picked her up, I was surprised how light she was—then I put her in the hole, and covered her over, though it was almost too dark to see by then.

The air smells very bad now, even in the Library, and worse every day—as if it is diseased itself, not just carrying disease—as if it is decaying into poison, maybe it is—and all the time it looks thickish and dirty, even in the middle of the day it's like a pale brown mist seeping into everything. What is the cause of this? This AIMD, what some of the reporters on TV called a 'plague' or a 'malignant virus'— Some religious nuts said that it's God's vengeance for mankind's evil, especially because of allowing homosexuality and same-sex marriage—and some of them said that AIMD was predicted in the Bible. Anyway, it started two years ago, and began to spread round the world very quickly, like the pandemics that happened a few years before that—the pandemics that killed so many millions of people, especially in Africa and South America and China and India, after the severe earthquakes and tornadoes and floods and tsunamis and the weird weather all round the world—but they said AIMD is even worse than those earlier pandemics because it kills so quickly, and spreads so quickly, and somehow it seems to be connected with the brown mist—but none of the scientists anywhere have been able to isolate or define it or discover exactly what causes it, so there are no pills or injections to cure it. If it *is* a virus, they say it might have originated in the Congo like Ebola and maybe AIDS, in gorillas and chimpanzees, and then jumped across to humans like they say AIDS did. But Dad, he said the air could just have been poisoned by all the pollution that has accumulated all round the world for so long, and that was the main cause—and he said how in the nineteenth-century people thought malaria came from bad air, that's why malaria is called that—but maybe they should have kept that name for AIMD, he said, with one of his sad smiles, or maybe AIMD should be called 'The Brown Death'. People who got sick with it, more and more and more of them, they couldn't be treated, they just sickened and died, like Mum did, and animals and plants are dying too and no medical experts seem to understand it, and no medical system in any country has been able to cope with it at all, especially now that antibiotics and other drugs can't help. So that's how it is—suffering and death are in control of us now, right round the world—suffering and death, not life and health and happiness like before—and none of us know how to exist this way. Assuming that anyone else does still exist! The University closed last month, not long after Dad's death and just two weeks before the end of the first term—many students had gone home already, and even faculty and staff were leaving—I wonder where they ended up, and whether they're all dead now. —But I know the rumour went round that the only way to avoid getting AIMD was to go into the countryside, far from cities, and they were saying that it hadn't reached the north and west of Canada. So now I think I've written down all I know about AIMD—oh and its name is an acronym of course, for 'Anti-Immune Mystery Disease'. Why didn't *I* get it, I wonder? I guess I still could. Surely I'm not immune? How could I be?

That Ted, he hated me—why am I thinking of him? Soon after he started in the Library, he was always watching me—sometimes I saw him checking, when he thought I wouldn't notice, to see if I had put books back in their right place, and of course I had, I was always very careful about that—there's nothing worse for a reader than not to be able to find a book on the shelves because it's been misplaced, I know that from experience. Sometimes there were official complaints from professors that they couldn't locate some book that they needed, and then there would be a fuss, we would be summoned and lectured and told to be more careful—and because of being the University Librarian's son, I had to be extra-careful anyway, so Ted didn't have evidence to accuse me of doing anything wrong—I knew that's what he wanted to do. He once said quietly to me "Of course you are fucking *special*, aren't you—you're protected, not like the rest of us—*we* make a slip, we're in trouble, but *you,* you fucking always get away with it." I didn't reply, I never did if anyone said anything like that to me—Dad always said it was better not to answer back, some people are just mean and hostile, best to ignore them. But then one late afternoon, just before closing-time, I was finishing replacing some PN books, right in the far corner of the fifth floor, when Ted comes up behind me, and puts an arm tight round me, and kisses my neck, and one of his hands slips down to my crotch. I said "No, don't do that, I don't want that" and twisted away from him. He said "Of course you want that, I've seen you looking at me, who do you think you're fucking fooling!" but I just put the last book in its place and walked away, pushing the empty cart. I know that women don't find me attractive in that way, not even Elise, but I don't want sex with men, especially after what Uncle Andrew did to me—Dad, when I told him about that, he said "I'll make sure that man is never alone with you again"—Mum and Dad, I don't think they really believed everything I told them—but Uncle Andrew didn't get a chance to kill me as he said he would if I ever told them, Dad sent him away. I knew that Ted was very angry with me, especially after I walked away from him like that, and that he wouldn't stop trying to hurt me. Then when Dad retired and the new Librarian took over, Ted had his opportunity—and he had got himself elected to some position in the Union too by then. I don't know exactly what he did and said, and who to, but I was 'let go'—I got a letter that said my position was being 're-evaluated'. I wanted to appeal, but Dad said "No, don't do that, it'll only cause you more pain and difficulty. Believe me, they need you, you're known to be careful and diligent, and they're always short of staff to do that work, they can't keep up with replacing books, you've seen that. Offer to be a volunteer and I'll pay you what you would have earned." So I stayed on, and avoided Ted as much as possible—but he was fired himself later, for insubordination, after the new Librarian saw him smoking weed in the stacks, that was the rumour anyway— someone told me that, and also told me that Dad didn't just retire, he was forced to retire, but I didn't believe that. So I applied to get my job back, and I did.

This afternoon I went up on the roof. I had never done that before, and I wasn't even sure how you could get up there, but I knew the west stairway went up from the sixth floor to the seventh, and ended at a locked brown steel door. I knew where the Library keys were too, behind the main desk, and when I tried them, one of them fit. I just wanted to see what I could, and especially if there was any sign of life on the campus. After- wards I had to sit on the stairs coming down, for quite a while, because I was so breathless, and also I felt nauseous—from emo- tion more than exhaustion—or the bad air, maybe. Up there it was hard to see anything much—even our house, only a short distance away, I could hardly see its shape through the murk— and beyond that, looking east toward the city and the lake, it was all brownish, like a flat screen with almost nothing showing through it—and silence, silence. No wind, not even the slightest breeze. After a few minutes up there, I began to feel shivery, and sad, and worried and depressed. I was also wondering how can I find out definitely if there is any life in all those nearby streets and houses that I knew so well during my boyhood, when I would often ride around on my bike? Are they all dead, all those neighbors and friends, or have they all gone away to try to escape AIMD? What of the stores in the centre of Westgreen Village, our suburb—are any of them open and functioning? Is there any life left at all here, in this whole area? That's what I was thinking. So now I am getting even more depressed. When I started writing again, after going up on the roof, this notebook fell open at the first words I wrote in it, and I thought how stupid I was then, and childish and naive, just a few days ago, to feel excitement, and almost pride, about maybe being the last person alive. It's just a cliché too, isn't it? —'The last man on earth'! Now I feel only horror when I think about it—that I could actually *be* the last person alive, and if so I must die alone, all alone.

Elise, she was my best friend—actually my only close friend. I could talk to her openly about all my thoughts and feelings, and did. How I wish, wish, wish she was here now! Where is she, is she still alive? Her parents came even before the University closed, and made her pack just a few clothes and leave with them immediately, they seemed to be in a panic—she was an only child and they lived in Toronto, but she said they were going to go to Northern Alberta, one of her uncles owned a ranch there. —She came rushing into the Library to tell me this, and it was lucky that I was at the main desk, where I sometimes worked if needed, and wasn't working that morning in the stacks. We only had time to gabble a few words while I walked out with her to the car—her parents were so impatient to leave that they hardly said a word to me when she introduced me to them—her father got out to open a back door for Elise, her mother just looked away into the distance. Elise turned to me before she got in, and smiled her wide curly smile, and blinked, the way she did when she smiled, I always loved seeing that. "We'll be in touch, hey—look after yourself, and remember Heraclitus!" —she said this softly so only I could hear, just before her father shut her into the back seat. We didn't have a chance to kiss or hug, or even shake hands, but I don't think we would have anyway, we weren't demonstrative like that—and I didn't even think I was in love with her until after she'd gone, and of course we haven't been able to communicate since then, I don't even know where she is. She smiled again and made a face and waved as the car drove off, and that's the last time I saw her. But I knew what she meant by 'remember Heraclitus'—he's our favourite early Greek philosopher, we especially admired him and often discussed five of his Fragments—"The world was always, is now, and always will be, everlasting fire" and "Fire lives the death of air, air lives the death of fire—water lives the death of earth, earth lives the death of water" and "You cannot step twice into the same river; for fresh waters are always flowing upon you" and "The way up and the way down are one and the same" and "We are, and are not." Elise and I argued interminably about what the Heraclitus Fragments really mean, trying to shake out their significance. She could be so sharp and fierce—I remember once she attacked me suddenly with "You know what 'philosophy' means, don't you? I sure *hope* so"—and I answered "Yes, of course I do, it's 'Seeking wisdom, and knowledge of all things and their causes'—from the Greek for love, *philos*, plus s*ophia*, wisdom." "So let's do it," she retorted, "let's stop faffing around, talking about things that don't matter. —So what do you think that actually *means*, what he says here?" And we were off! Another time, she suddenly said "And what about the women, do you ever think of *them*? I guess you don't" and I said "What do you mean?" and she said "Doesn't it ever occur to you that early

Greek *women* might have been interested in the nature of reality, and maybe it was *Mrs* Leucippus who, between having babies and feeding her husband and cleaning the house, told him her theory that *atoms* are the beginning and end of all things—after all, that's how women live their lives, don't they? experiencing the nature of reality every moment of every day in millions of small events. And her atomic theory was the most important of them all, the beginning of Science—and of course *Mr* Leucippus got the credit for it."

Oh, Elise! Lovely Elise. I remember so vividly where, when and how we met. I was re-shelving books in B, the philosophy section, when this dark petite first-year student comes up to me and says "Please could you help me, if you have the time? I can't find a book I want, and yet it should be here—I checked the computer to see if it was out, and it's not, and it's not on reserve, so it should be here, right here, but it isn't." Usually I would have said something like "I'm sorry, you'll have to fill in a lost-book search form at the main desk and they'll try to locate it for you." But for some reason, maybe her polite determination and that wide smile, I went across to where she was looking for it. She handed me a slip of paper with the call-number on it: B171.R66—I've just taken the book from the shelf again, and held it, as both I and Elise held it that afternoon, when I gave it to her—*Retrieving the Ancients: An Introduction to Greek Philosophy* by David Roochnik—a strange surname, Russian maybe? Of course she had been right, the book wasn't where it should have been, but I also thought it wouldn't have been misplaced in the way that, say, PR books are sometimes misplaced in BR or DF or FR, and disappear for ever! So I told her to follow me across to the 'Books to be Re-shelved' section—and yes, there it was! She was so delighted, so grateful, that I felt embarrassed. When she suddenly said "Please come and have a coffee with me, can you,

I'd really like that," I answered just as impulsively, to my own surprise, "Well, I guess I could, after I go off duty," and so we had our first conversation, in the Student Centre—she insisted on paying for the coffees of course, that afternoon, but then I paid the next time, and soon it was a regular meeting, and I could see that she enjoyed our get-togethers too. For the first time ever, I actually felt at ease with another person! She told me she was a first-year student, intending to major in philosophy and psychology, and then train to be a psychiatrist like her father. She was an Ontario Scholar, with a high-school grade-average of A+, but I saw long before I knew those facts that she was brilliant, complex, confident, enthusiastic, open, honest, and—*unique*—but she also made *me* feel brilliant and unique, and for the first time in my life I had a great time talking, conversing, with another human being! I never felt closer to anyone, not even my Mother, although Elise and I were separated by more than twenty years—she was 18 when we met, and I was 39, over twice her age!—and we're so different from each other in so many ways—but somehow we are united, we are *one*, in a very deep and mysterious way, and always will be—at least that's what I believe! I'm so grateful to her, and to have known her, that sometimes, like now, I feel like weeping with happiness and pain—pain and happiness.

As you can see, this notebook is almost full! I think I know where I'll find some others—in the 'Lost and Found' drawer at the main desk—students are always forgetting possessions in the stacks or wherever, and that drawer is where small items like ballpoints and iPhones and notebooks end up waiting to be claimed, and mostly they aren't—and it's amazing how many big items, even coats and laptops, also get left behind and never claimed—I wonder what happens to them in the end? I've written so many words in this one notebook—it's becoming a sort of diary without dates. As Heraclitus might have said, "Rivers flow onwards, but all is one." Whatever that means! Elise and I were first united by a mutual fascination with those early Greek philosophers, to whom she introduced me during our conversation in the Student Centre that afternoon. While we drank our coffees, she told me that the first lecture in her Intro Philosophy course, just that morning, had started with a few quotations from those philosophers, and she had immediately decided to find out as much as possible about them and their ideas—they were unique, those philosophers, she said—they were the first human beings, at least in our Western society, to try to understand the nature of the world we inhabit, its meaning, and the meaning of our existence in it—the world that may now be doomed, as we its creatures seem to be doomed. Is it truly The End, as you said, Dad? Or a new beginning?

II

Two notebooks—in the 'Lost and Found' drawer I found two notebooks, both only slightly used by their previous owners—for lecture notes, mostly illegible to me. So here I go again, spewing my words onto naked pages, almost as if I am with Elise and we are arguing over what one of our early Greek philosophers might have said—and of course whatever that was, she would always remind me, it was originally expressed over two thousand years ago in ancient Greek, a language very different from English, and within a culture quite different from ours, even though it influenced ours so greatly—so how can we ever be sure about what exactly they said, let alone what they meant? The few words, miraculously surviving words, of those philosophers are preserved in only a few Fragments, quotations in the writings of successors—and they are precious, literally priceless, she would say, because they partially preserve the earliest human attempts to penetrate the essence of our existence and environment. Elise and I—in our earnest conversations, we tried to revive that ancient debate about the nature of reality, challenging the philosophers' speculations as well as each other's interpretations of them. Thales, he was the granddaddy of them all, but why did he decide that "the first principle of things is water"? —"Well, of course," Elise might say, "he was surrounded by water, the Mediterranean enfolded the whole known world" and I'd object "But what about rocks and trees, didn't he think they existed too?" and on we'd go. Anaximander, no, no, not water, but a mysterious infinite substance—Anaximenes, air, it's air, stupid, our souls are air, the earth is encompassed by air, it's all air—Pythagoras, mathematical structure, numbers, harmony of opposites, all things composed of five solidities, I avoided him as much as possible because his insights were somehow too diverse and complex for me—Xenophanes, I can't recall what he thought—Parmenides, no, not air or fire or earth or water, or even all four elements interacting, no, the universe just *is* what it *is*, as if that's any sort of answer—and Zeno, Melissus, Empedocles, Anaxagoras—Leucippus and Democritas the Atomists, who got it right with their jostling atoms, or did they?—Protagoras, Gorgias, Thrasymachus, Callicles, Critias—how I relish their names! In fact I confess that I remember their names better than their theories. Those thinkers of the distant past, they all contributed their answers to the greatest and most basic of human questions, and finally their big guy arrived, the hugely ambitious philosopher who stood on top of all their theories and reached for universal fame—tragic Socrates, who with his admiring disciple and successor Plato changed the channel, or rather widened it beyond metaphysics to include social issues, ethics, aesthetics, politics, the whole range of speculation and analysis we now call philosophy. Elise and I, we never thought what some of her fellow-students thought, that the early Greek philosophers' debate about the nature of reality was boring, irrelevant or inconsequential—we loved it with a passion, and were deeply moved by the very conception of those men struggling, so long ago, to understand the world around them, each of them yearning for conclusive insight and knowledge—and all without the aid of textbooks and encyclopedias and the Internet, advantages we their successors have possessed, through our ever-advancing technology and easy rapid communication. They had only their minds, their bare minds—oh, but that was enough for Elise and me, we were enchanted by their endless curiosity, as we tussled our own way through thickets of confusion and doubt, always hoping but always failing to achieve anything like certainty ourselves. We also recognized, I think, that those men, simple and harsh though their lives were, compared to ours—often in dangerous political circumstances or in tenuous isolated communities clinging to inhospitable mountains and valleys—yet demonstrated more respect, more humility and appreciation and gratitude for the world we inhabit, than we, latter-day despoilers, we ultimate tragedians, have done. And so my lecture ends!

I decided last night, while I was trying and failing to get some sleep, that as soon as possible I *must* go on an expedition into Westgreen, to see if there are any signs of life there. I need to *know*. Am I truly the only living inhabitant of this suburb and this university campus? I am beginning to feel mentally as well as physically sick, and increasingly lonely and frightened. Maybe there's no hope of worthwhile existence left and I will soon be only too glad to die, of AIMD or despair, or even by my own hand. But first, while I am still capable, and if only in the spirit of the enquiry Elise and I initiated, I must make an effort to understand my situation. The nature of *my* reality! So this morning I emerged from the Library, and explored the University buildings opposite—intending to assure myself that there are no people in them, and so probably in the entire campus, before I set off to explore Westgreen. I locked the Library's main door as I left—why? The doors into the Student Centre weren't locked, so I went inside and wandered around its ground floor, once crowded with students hurrying to lectures or meeting friends for coffee or lunch. Now empty and silent, so silent. The restaurants, the travel agency, the drugstore, the information booth, all neatly closed and secured, looking so ordinarily ready to re-open tomorrow morning and resume serving their student-customers. I climbed the stairs—the lifts weren't working of course, just like those in the Library—and looked briefly into several student-group offices. Silence, silence. Downstairs, and over into the linked Administration Building, and along a broad passage, and past various offices once busily occupied by secretaries and other staff, now all equally and dispiritingly neat, clean and silent. To the Bookstore, where I had seen lights glowing for days after the University's closure—no lights now, all the doors locked, and through the glass of the main door, I could see, beyond the racks of clothes, rows and rows of shiny new computers. By this point, depression was threatening to overwhelm me, so I went back to the Student Centre and sat for a few minutes at the table where Elise and I once sat—and tried to restore my composure, if not achieve a sliver of optimism. How *could* I feel optimistic? Yet to settle into despair— But then why should one resist despair? Because to accept despair is demeaning, unnatural? But why? —Merely because one is alive, and life insists that one should go on being alive as long as possible? "Keep right on to the end of the road"—Harry Lauder, Mum used to have a crackly old 78 rpm record of him singing that mournful song, and I have a childhood memory of her playing it on an ancient record-player and singing along in her thin voice while cooking—she had inherited that and other records from her very Scottish mother, the grandmother I never knew, who died before I was born. So go on, keep right on to the end, I told myself, and don't again ask why, for there can be no answer. After a couple of hours, I decided there was no point looking for any further signs of life in those buildings or elsewhere on the campus, which seemed to have been evacuated in as orderly a way as one might hope, during the time I was preoccupied with Dad's death and then Mum's illness and death. The whole University seems to be waiting to be reopened and re-occupied—apparently ready to swing straight back into life. But for now, and maybe for ever, it is lifeless. So I came back to the Library and opened a couple of cans for my lunch, and wrote down more words in this notebook, the words you have just been reading if you are reading *these* words—and while I ate and drank, I tried to encourage myself to get ready to set off on an expedition into Westgreen.

Elise and I, we were a team. 'A team of two'. That's what she said once, when I was trying to help her while she was studying for her Intro Philosophy exam. She had a superb memory—could recall accurately not only names and dates, but also, word for word, what each of the early Greek philosophers said, or was said to have said—we would compete, and play memory games too, and laugh and laugh! Elise and I. She changed my life for the better, and I wish so very much that she was still here and we could get together again and talk—and it just came to me that maybe I should write this for her, this 'diary without dates', write it as if I'm talking to her! So this is all for you, Ell! I'm writing it for you, wherever you are, it's a sort of letter to say that I hope you are still alive, and that we will be able to be together again before long, and meanwhile I'm recording how my life goes since you left. As I think I wrote earlier, there was never anything sexual in our companionship—or, if there was, it was buried deep within our psyches. I assume that you agree, Ell! You had a boyfriend and I would see him sometimes, briefly, when I came to meet you in the late afternoon—he was usually there, sitting close beside you, but when he saw me approaching he would jump up and leave. Once I said to you "Don't you think Abdul would like to stay and join in our conversation, I'd like that, wouldn't you?" but you were decisive as always, "No, he's not into philosophical conjectures, he's an engineer, he and I just enjoy socializing and dancing together"— and making love, I added silently to myself, for it was obvious to me that you and he were physically at ease with each other, and twice, as I turned the corner, I glimpsed him kissing you and holding you hard against him. His sudden departures suggested that he might be nervous of me, maybe because I was 'different', a strange older male, not a youthful student like him, and not a prof—hard to place. He was a very beautiful young man, slim and golden and intense—an Iranian, you told me, grandson of a self-exiled politician. And you are Jewish, Ell, the only child of a wealthy Toronto psychiatrist, and niece of a rabbi. That wasn't a problem for me, your relationship with Abdul, as I hope you recognized—I wasn't jealous, in fact I respected both of you for rising above the antipathy between your inherited cultures and histories, and for expressing openly your maturity, sensitivity, and optimistic political ideals— though it seemed obvious to me that sexual attraction and enjoyment were the most powerful forces holding the two of you together. Am I right? After you and I had been meeting and talking philosophy for several weeks, and I had noted your involvement with Abdul, I thought you might begin to lose interest in our get-togethers and tell me you were moving on, and so I began preparing myself for disappointment—after all, apart from spending time with Abdul, you were busy with several other courses, and with other activities too, like your work for Amnesty International and animal rights and the environment—you always teased me about being 'right-wing', 'nauseatingly conservative' you said once, and I guess I am, compared to you! But no—we didn't stop meeting, and our conversations never flagged.

Heraclitus. Why, of all the early philosophers, did we find him so attractive, talk so much about his ideas? Among the reasons, I think, was a literary reference I made during one of our discussions. I had half-remembered a poem, which must have been in one of Mum's poetry anthologies—she probably read it to me herself, for I was a nervous child and often had difficulty getting to sleep, imagining monsters lurking in the room's dark corners, so she would read poems to me until my eyes closed—I still recall them occasionally, unexpectedly. On that occasion with Elise, quite spontaneously I recited "They told me, Heraclitus, they told me you were dead, / They brought me bitter news to hear, and bitter tears to shed." I remember how you pulled back and scrutinized me, and said "Wow! Cool! Where'd that come from? It's beautiful, say it again", and I did—and then I recalled two other lines from the poem—which turned out, when I checked later in the *Oxford Book of Quotations*, to be by an obscure nineteenth-century English poet called Cory—"How often you and I / Had tired the sun with talking and sent him down the sky." That became a little joke with us—you or I would end a conversation with "So now, have we tired the sun with talking and sent him down the sky?" And I also remembered that T.S. Eliot had been fascinated by Heraclitus and in *The Four Quartets* had quoted one of the insights Elise and I were struggling with, "The way up is the way down, the way forward is the way back"—I hadn't read Eliot's poem for a while, but that night I located it on my poetry shelf and re-read the whole of it. Dad was very ill and in hospital by then, after his first heart attack—and I remember how consoling I found reading that poem. You had also asked if I knew any other English poems that quoted or referred to the early Greek philosophers, and later I remembered the title "Empedocles on Etna" and dug up that poem, it's by Matthew Arnold—we read it aloud together, but you kept giggling at the pretentious style, and we quickly realized too that the whole poem was set up to praise the poet, Callicles, and sneer at his 'opposite', Empedocles the philosopher, who of course finally yields to despair and commits suicide by plunging into the crater of Mount Etna—"we shall feel our powers of effort flag, / And rally them for one last fight—and fail . . ." No, we were not impressed by that poem, and especially by the way it cast the philosopher and poet as opposites, enemies—"He's creating and exploiting a false dichotomy" you said— But I remember we both liked a few lines, even as we also ridiculed them—"Is it so small a thing / To have enjoyed the sun, / To have lived light in the spring, / To have loved, to have thought, to have done?" I guess I was thinking of Dad too, I'd seen him the night before— he'd seemed close to death, lying silent and drugged in his hospital bed, while Mum and I sat beside him holding hands, silent too. Then you suddenly asked "And what other poetic

Fragments do you have crawling around inside that rapidly balding cranium of yours? You are so secretive! Who is your favourite poet? What is your favourite poem? Do you write poetry?" And I was ready to answer all three of those questions if we'd been able to meet again. But of course there was no opportunity before you rushed breathless up to me in the Library and told me your parents were taking you away.

Well, I did go on my journey into Westgreen, yesterday afternoon, two days after I first intended. I also set off later than intended, at about two o'clock—and the whole experience has been traumatic. I feel stupid writing that, 'traumatic', since I'm the only reader of this—and I know what happened of course, so why bother to record my reaction? Last time I wrote in this notebook, it really felt as if Elise was with me and we were sitting together—my mind was turbulent with emotion, about Dad dying and Mum weeping silently, and the poetry, and Heraclitus, and above all Elise herself—I was remembering our lovely relationship, and I wanted so deeply to tell her what has been happening to me. But I guess that was self-deception—in reality I am writing this for myself, as I said earlier, and I'm also wondering if it's just a waste of time and energy, if there is any point in writing it at all, but I guess that at the very least it gives me a distracting occupation—and also there is a remote possibility that strangers may eventually read these words, so maybe I should try to make what I write as accurate and detailed as possible—just in case these words, *my* Fragments, survive into the future, if there is one—then maybe two readers like Elise and me will come across my Fragments, and argue over what they mean—assuming, if it's very far in the future, that the English language will not have changed too radically, or even have fallen out of use and so need to be translated! It was Mum who first got me to keep a diary, though I didn't do it for very long—she told me she kept one herself when she was a girl, and that it had improved her 'writing skills'—of course I wanted to read it, but she laughed and said she hadn't had time to continue writing it after she got married, "it never left Scotland, I don't know what happened to it, my mother probably found it and burnt it—Andrew told me she destroyed 'everything she could' before she died."

Anyway, by the time I set out on my journey of discovery, quite a strong wind was, surprisingly, blowing from the west—no problem when I walked towards the centre of Westgreen, but when I was walking back here later, it pushed hard at me and slashed at my face. Of course it brought no rain, only dust, and the air still stank, but not so noticeably, or maybe I am getting used to it now. I tried to scrutinize every house as I passed by, walking slowly along the road. The afternoon was darkening already under the heavy grey clouds. No lights in the houses, of course, and no movement except when the wind flapped a flag that was still hanging on a pole outside one of the houses, or blew dust or scraps of paper or dead leaves past my feet. I didn't feel quite as frightened as I had expected, but it was eerie all the same, because of the silence, the gloom, and the apparent absence of life—even the trees all dead or dying. I wondered if any of the houses had corpses in them, but I didn't try to investigate—that would have felt like an illegal intrusion, and could have been very scary too. Occasionally I would think I glimpsed a shape or movement in a room behind a window, and would stop to look closely—but no, only ghosts maybe, though I don't believe in ghosts. As I passed one house, I noticed a movement inside what seemed to be its living room, as if a person had moved jerkily from one side of the room to the other—so I approached the house slowly and carefully along its crazy-paving pathway, and stepped sideways when I was close to the porch, to look into the room—and found I was looking directly at a smudged torso, and a grey head that wiggled and wavered until, suddenly, it transmogrified into mine, my mirrored wide-open eyes and gaping black mouth—and only then my bated breath broke free in a relieved gasp.

Still walking very slowly, I came to the major intersection so familiar to me, and turned left onto the main street through the centre of Westgreen, where the stores begin—the traffic lights at the intersection creaked softly in the wind, they weren't functioning of course, were merely blank holes, blind eyes. This made me recall a scene at the start of one of those Dickens movies I saw on video when I was a boy—*Great Expectations* maybe, when Pip encounters Magwitch among the gravestones in the spooky churchyard—but of course many horror movies had scenes like that, and it felt almost as if I was in a horror movie anyway. I walked on steadily, in the middle of the main street, passing the long-familiar buildings on each side—the bank where I used to cash checks and collect money from the machines, the drugstore where I used to buy toothpaste and Tylenols, the cinema where I had seen a few movies over the years, the pub where I used to go for lunch and a beer occasionally. Only two vehicles were parked along the road— side by side outside the pub—a new-looking small blue car, and an unkempt green truck with bulging brown sacks loaded in the back, surely a farmer's truck. I walked over to the pub and tried the big red front door, which pulled open easily, soundlessly. Going inside to the second door, I became very aware of warm air and a sharp sickly smell—the smell, it must be, of putrefaction, the smell which had become noticeable earlier, though more faintly, in occasional whiffs while I was walking past houses—but now, when I opened the inner door of the pub, the smell struck me full in the face, and I recoiled, after gazing briefly at the bodies of a man and woman, slumped together on stools at the bar counter, their backs to me—she wearing a white T-shirt and pale-blue skirt, he a red-and-green checked shirt and tan trousers, his left arm draped across her shoulders, his right one cradling a half-full glass of beer, both his arms bare and dark brown—and their heads, his hair short and fair, hers long and auburn, laid side by side on the counter. I was glad I couldn't see their faces, and glad to turn away from them, and leave the pub, closing its big red door carefully behind me. How had they died so tidily together?

I walked a short way along one of the service roads behind the row of stores on my right, noticing a small delivery-truck parked near one of them, and a child's tricycle on its side at the back door of another. Yes, it was weird, exploring the centre of Westgreen—and what I'd seen suddenly reminded me of a particular opening scene—the movie was *The Last Man on Earth*, one of three on a DVD of 'classic horror movies' that I picked up, about twenty years ago, in a garage sale. —But of course in Westgreen there are no corpses in the streets, and I'm no Vincent Price, and I sure hope there are no vampires gathering to attack me tonight! How can I joke about such things? But recalling that old horror movie makes me think that maybe some memories of it were at the back of my mind when I started to keep this 'diary without dates'—the movie's title, at least, and that the Vincent Price character was the only survivor of some plague that had wiped out most of humanity— I remember expecting that he would ultimately be provided with a well-endowed mate so they could repopulate the Earth, after all it was a Hollywood B-movie, wasn't it? But it ended tragically, the Last Survivor became a Non-Survivor. As I walked back through the centre of Westgreen, I also thought of the "Sleeping Beauty" fairy tale, a favourite of my childhood, maybe of most childhoods—how everyone and everything had been cursed, stricken motionless, waiting for the prince to arrive so he could kiss the princess and then life could resume. A horror movie and a fairy tale! Childish—I am so immature!

This is reality, actuality, what I am experiencing—however strange and unreal it seems, however close to cliché. Time to go. Darkness is imminent. I can't say I felt much emotion, apart from relief—earlier I had been fearful, cowardly, I admit that—but I guess I also felt disappointed, empty, as I left the centre of Westgreen and walked back towards the Library as fast as I could, into the buffeting wind.

As I walked, I found that I was thinking again about the dead man and woman in the pub. Who were they, why were they there? The two vehicles parked outside suggested a rendezvous. Were they secret lovers who had met in the pub and returned there in the end, only to die together, after all or most of the local population had departed? —he a pub 'regular', she a barmaid? Or had he arrived to take her with him to his farm—but neither knowing they were already infected with the Brown Death? Or maybe they had committed suicide together by drinking beer that they had poisoned? I imagined the two entwined corpses sitting there in the pub forever, forever—slowly mouldering into a dusty eternity—silent, silent. And then I started meditating on silence itself, the various types or dimensions of silence—how the silence of the dead lovers, the silence of Westgreen, the silence in the University's Student Centre and administrative offices, was so disturbing, threatening, frightening, since it seemed so unnatural, and signified the absence of a life-force that, not long before, had pulsed strongly there. And how, in contrast, the silence of the Library did not so much threaten as calm and console me, since it had become established, during my long experience working there, as natural, and ideal, positive. And what about our house, my ex-home, emptied of my parents and Thumper but, like the Library, a guardian of my history, my past? After the departure of Fiona, it had become a quiet place—but not silent, as it is now. Yes, and the silence there had made me uneasy, in its unfamiliarity and ambiguity—had promoted, surely, my decision to live in the Library. So why did I go there again—to the house, the home of my past? I hadn't really intended to—but I would pass close by it on my way back to the Library, and I was certainly feeling tired after trudging around Westgreen and struggling against the gusty dry wind, and it would be a familiar and comfortable refuge, I could sit and rest for half-an-hour on the couch in the silent living room—and who knows, I guess I was thinking that it might also be my last visit there, the familiar place where I grew up. And I had suddenly remembered that Dad kept a flashlight in the basement that might be useful at night in the Library. Though it was beginning to get much darker now—for the time was about half-past four according to my watch—I thought it was still light enough for a short visit to the house if I didn't linger there before going across the road to the Campus—I knew the way so well, anyway, and wouldn't have any problem unlocking the main Library door even in total darkness, if Dad's flashlight wasn't in its usual place after all.

The side door of our house was closest to the stairs down to the basement, so I unlocked it and entered the house that way. Silence, silence. I felt my way down the stairs very carefully, in the semi-darkness, found the flashlight, and with it lighted my way back up. As I reached the top of the stairs—was that a sound? I stood there, tense, my heart actually beating fast. After a few moments, a sudden brief scratchy scuttering sound near the back door! My heart really jumped then, the noise was so unexpected in the midst of all that thick silence. Was it something blown down by the wind? I crept very carefully towards the kitchen window, to look out onto the deck, and there it was. *He* was. Of course. Next-door's big black cat. The murderous Mr Death, as I had named him. Emaciated—and his pale green eyes staring at me out of the dusk. He was squatted on a plastic table just outside the kitchen window, and had clearly scratched and pummeled the window, after hearing me open the side door and walk about in the house. Anger almost choked me as I remembered how he had killed and eaten my beloved Thumper. I didn't write about that earlier—I guess because the whole episode upset me so much that I wanted to sweep it out of my mind, forget about it completely. But here he was. Murderer of Thumper and loathed destroyer of so many birds that Mum's birdseed had attracted, before she stopped feeding them to avoid sentencing them to sudden death in his jaws. So now we glared at each other, the cat and I, while I heard again that pitiful squeal of pain, and turned with Mum's body in my arms to see Thumper being dragged to his destruction under the deck—there was nothing I could do to save him, unless I had dropped Mum's body and tried to pursue the cat and his victim into the low dark dirty space under our deck, and I couldn't and didn't do that. While I was burying Mum, I could hear Thumper's body being cracked open and his flesh consumed—it was agonizing to try not to hear what was happening, so close and so far. Of course Thumper's death was partly my fault, to the extent that I had forgotten he was in the kitchen, so that, when I propped open the back door to carry Mum's body to the grave I had dug, he could easily follow us— and I'm convinced that he followed us because of his love for Mum, a thought that greatly increased my anger against Mr Death. Next day, the day after burying Mum, I located Thumper's pathetic few bones under the deck, so that I could at least bury those beside her. But now—what to do about Mr Death? I considered running out onto the deck with the broom and attacking and hopefully killing him—but, apart from a squeamish reluctance to be quite so violent and destructive, I told myself that it would be foolish to put myself at risk of falling, or of being attacked by the obviously starving creature, and scratched by his probably infected claws. So, in the end, Thumper went unavenged. I even opened a can of sardines and pushed it out through the back doorway and onto the deck, together with a bowl of water. Forgiveness was not possible, but I reminded myself about the baleful nature of cats, and told myself that Mr Death could not reasonably be blamed for his unfortunate inheritance. What do you think of that, as an example of benign practical philosophy, Ell—do you approve? Just as humans are condemned to be inquisitive and creative, in your view—so cats are condemned to slaughter birds and mice. —Oh, I'm being facetious now, but I confess that, after I'd got over the shock of his appearance, I actually found some relief from the loneliness and depression of my situation in this encounter with Mr Death, the only other creature, as far as I knew, keeping me company, however temporarily, in these probably final days. He did not choose me, I certainly did not choose him, the murderous brute—but there we were, together, the two of us. I guess I will come back and feed him again— that's what I was thinking, when the second shock fell upon me.

After I had pushed the opened can of sardines and bowl of water out on the deck, and seen Mr Death throw himself upon them, I decided it would be safe for me to leave, again by the side door. It was now almost pitch-dark. I knew that with the flashlight I would have no difficulty at all in reaching and unlocking the main Library door, and then finding my way to the University Librarian's Office—but still I felt anxious to get there quickly, no doubt I was still a bit unnerved by the West-green expedition and the shock of Mr Death's appearance. So I hurried out, locked the door, and switched the flashlight on as I turned. It's difficult now to recall and describe the series of rapid events that ensued, and my appalled reactions to them. First, I think I noticed, from the corner of my eyes, that Next-door's outer door was propped open—his side entrance is directly opposite ours, about ten feet away, just across the driveway. I took a hesitant impulsive step backwards.   And then—then I noticed that the inner door was slightly ajar, and through its small window a shadow was growing. —And as my flashlight swung from side to side, the shadow became a wavering indistinct outline of shoulders and neck and shrouded head—the torso of a vampire—or ghost— But by then the inner door was opening and he was in full sight, turning his face away from the glare of my flashlight. —Yes, it was Next-door, it was flesh and blood, he was gesturing, and I heard him calling out, gruff and a bit muffled, "Come in, for Heaven's sake come in here." After a moment, and feeling both shaky and foolish, I went across to speak to him. "Come in, come in" he reiterated. I stumbled on the lintel as I stepped jerkily into his passageway and nearly fell against him. Dr Benjamin Bowman, Professor of English Literature—yes, of course I knew who he was, had often seen him and exchanged a few brief neighbourly words over the years, had even once or twice served him at the main desk of the Library. "Hi" I said feebly. "My dear boy, I hope I didn't startle you," he responded, taking off the white face-mask that had made him look so other-worldly. "I've seen you going in or out of your house quite a few times since the University closed, and since—your Father's death, so I—and your Mother's too, it's all so horrific, what's happening now, isn't it?—so I wanted to make contact, and see if I could, you know, help. —Do you want to come in and partake of a meal with me? you'd be very welcome—I can't offer anything very appetizing, I'm afraid, it'll be out of cans, but I do have some wine to help it go down smoothly—so—" "Oh, no," I said immediately and, in the circumstances, rather stupidly—the whole situation seemed quite surrealistic. "Thank you very much, Dr Bowman, but I'm all right, I'm just on my way to the Library." Even my voice sounded odd. "To the Library?" he asked, surprised. "*Now?* Surely it's closed, like the rest of the University? And why would you go there now anyway, at this time of day?" "Well—that's where—I'm living there, you see—since my parents died—" He looked hard at me, quizzically.

"Well, anyway, let's not stand here with the door open—I see you have a flashlight, and here, I have one too, follow me" as he switched his on and started slowly down the basement stairs—but still I demurred, "No, really, thank you, but I must get back to the Library." He half-turned to look back up at me. "Well, I can't force you, can I? But apart from trying to help you if I can—I owe your Father that, and your Mother—there are some things I would very much like to talk to you about, important things. I've been downstairs in the basement most of the time recently—in fact I only ever come upstairs to sleep, or get a book from my office—since everything closed down on the Campus, and all the students disappeared, even the two gradu- ate students whose dissertations I'm supervising, they didn't call or e-mail me, they just went away, it seems—since then I've been concentrating on my book, I was determined to finish it, whatever happens, and I didn't want any interruptions—but now it's finished, just yesterday, the first draft, and I'm revising the text so that I can get it to the publisher in New York as soon as possible—and I'd like you to see two of the chapters, it's a stroke of luck that you're here this evening—it concerns you to some extent, some of the book does, as you'll see—" Voluble, gabbling. But he was interrupted by a coughing fit, and when it finished he stood clutching the rail, gasping for breath. "Well, I can't stop you going if you are so determined," he wheezed at last. "But let's talk more. Come tomorrow morning? Will you?" He pulled his face-mask out of a pocket, and fastened it back over his nose and mouth. "Yes, I'll come back tomorrow, Dr Bowman," I promised, speaking quickly but as calmly as I could, "I'll definitely come back tomorrow morning, but I must go now," and I went. I was thinking that I did not know or like this old man, did not want to spend time with him—but that those feelings were irrelevant now, he was a fellow survivor, and Fate had thrown us together, just as his bloody cat and I had been thrown together—and if I was coming back to feed his bloody cat next morning, then I might as well look in on his owner.

As I made my way to the Library in the darkness, I was surprised to feel almost cheerful—certainly no longer tense—for, after the fearful apprehension, then the distressing exploration of Westgreen, then the two shocks when I visited our house, the day seemed to be ending in an unexpected, even a positive, way. Too tired to think further, I could only feel relief and elation in a simple fact—that I am not the last man alive! I am not the last man alive. How stupid ever to think I was! When I reached Dad's couch, I fell onto it, pulled the blanket over my weary body, and almost simultaneously slipped into a deep, deep sleep.

III

I woke up early this morning, having slept well for the first time in weeks, and now feeling livelier and more optimistic. After eating a breakfast of pineapple slices and cookies, courtesy of my gradually dwindling store of food, I climbed the stairs up to the sixth floor to replace the early Greek philosophy book, the one that began my friendship with Elise—I had taken it down to the University Librarian's Office with me two days ago—why? Not to read it again, but I guess you could say to meditate over it, to inspire me to recall in detail that initial meeting and its consequences. After I'd replaced it, I went across to the re-shelving shelves, and saw that there were a good few other philosophy books lined up there, so I piled about twenty of them into a cart and replaced them on the shelves, realizing how wrong I was to write earlier, in the first notebook, that there was no re-shelving left to do—in fact, as I found when I went down to the fifth floor, where the largest number of books had always accumulated awaiting our attention—especially HCs and PNs!—there's actually enough work to keep me occupied for a while yet. I guess old habits die hard, or you could say long-inculcated employment duties cling to life— and if the Library is to be returned to its optimal state, ready at any moment to welcome new readers, I'm the only one here to do that! I am the University Librarian. I am! After I'd emptied the cart, it occurred to me that it was probably a good time for me to go across to Next-door, Dr Ben Bowman—I didn't much want to, but a promise is a promise—and it was 10 a.m., my watch was still efficiently tracking time, its tiny battery making it an example of one of the few modern mechanical marvels still able to function. While their batteries last, I guess radios, like computers, including Dr Bowman's laptop and his printer, also remain usable—but there is only silence or static on all the radio stations, which implies the breakdown of the relevant equipment or the absence of all personnel, or both. In that respect, I should record here that, alas, following the stoppage of water-flow a few weeks ago, no doubt because the whole Hydro system had broken down, the washroom I have been using has become increasingly malodorous owing to the impossibility of flushing my feces away—but fortunately the Library has a plethora of washrooms, more than I ever needed to notice, and all of them, men's and women's, are available to me! However, I have no way of bathing, and can wash myself only with small quantities of water from Dad's collection of bottled spring-water—he had filled several buckets of water for flushing the toilet in our house, but they were too heavy for me to lump over to the Library, so I am beginning to feel quite smelly myself. But what can I do about that? Try not to notice, I guess. Now I must stop writing and go across to Dr Bowman's house. But first I went back to the Librarian's Office with a heavy book by the famous British philosopher Bertrand Russell that I'd noticed and picked up while re-shelving philosophy books—his *History of Western Philosophy*, B72.R8. I left it on Dad's desk, for possible later reading.

It was still quite chilly and gloomy when I left the Library— will I ever see the sun again? —Of course its rays can't penetrate the roiling grey clouds that bulge so heavily above the dirty air that is making me cough more and more frequently. Even yesterday's wind brought no change in the air quality. Another absence in my life now is the daily weather forecast, once regular on the radio and TV—so now changes of weather are literally unpredictable, as they always were for everybody everywhere until comparatively recently, before our era—when

I guess one had to rely on uncertain signs derived from folk-lore, like my Mum's favourite "Red sky in the morning is the shepherd's warning, red sky at night is the shepherd's delight"—did that one actually work, I wonder, when there *were* sunrises and sunsets? I was outside Dr Bowman's side entrance by about 10:30. Just as I was opening the outer door, having found that it was unlocked, I felt, with a momentary shock, pressure against my left leg—I looked down, and there of course was Mr Death, twining his scrawny blackness against me. His entreaty was obvious, enhanced by hoarse purring, so I went into our house, preventing him from following, opened another can of sardines, pushed it out the back door, with a bowl of water, and saw him fall on it. "My truly inexplicable good deed for the day," I told him silently, then went over again to Next-door's side entrance. Like the outer door, the inner one was unlocked. As I pushed it open, calling out "Hi, hullo," I heard coughing from the basement. After a moment, his voice, hoarse and shaky, "I'm here, I'm here, come on down." Dr Bowman was sitting slumped in a large black leather armchair, with at least one blanket pulled right up to his chin. A candle flickered on the table beside him. More coughing, then "Bloody cold this morning, bloody cold," he grumbled—though I didn't think it was—"Sit down, sit down." I sat on the low office chair opposite him. "So you've come. I wondered if you would. But then I suppose you are as dutiful as your parents trained you to be." I laughed, uncomfortably, "Well—" "Listen, my dear, I've been thinking," he rasped, twisting his head as if his neck was causing him pain, "we haven't any time to waste, have we? That's if all they were saying has any credibility, the pundits I mean—and you would know that better than I, you've presumably been out and about at least occasionally, while I've been stuck down here, finishing my book and wondering and waiting, feeling more and more worried, wondering even if I should make the effort to get outside and explore the environs. Is there anyone else around—on the Campus, or anywhere in the vicinity? In any of the houses? Surely we two are not the only ones? I refuse to believe that. Whatever all those merchants of doom were saying on the news, when there *was* news—I've lost track of how long ago all that stopped, must be over a month ago? I must admit that I didn't pay a whole lot of attention before I finished the book"—he gestured at a pile of paper on a small table to his right—"but then the Hydro suddenly stopped, and darkness fell upon the land—and the radio's useless now, nothing but silence from it, or occasional squeaks and gibberish—and the cellphone and iphone etcetera etcetera, also useless, all of them—but thank goodness for my CD player—as long as the batteries last, I've already replaced one, and now I've only got three left, but I can still hear some of my favourite music—what a deprivation that would be, my dear, if I couldn't do that, almost worse than death that would be, ultimate isolation. And lucky that your Father and I stocked up when the scare began or I would have starved to death by now—how do *you* manage to survive?" "Well—also on the food and soup and juice and water that Dad stored in our basement. Even your cat, I was able to feed him yesterday and today from those cans." "*My* cat? You mean your Mother's cat, my dear." "Mum's cat? No, we never had a cat. I mean *your* one, the black one," and I almost added "the one who ate my rabbit." I was feeling more and more uncomfortable in Dr Ben Bowman's company, partly I think because of his hectoring manner and reiterated "my dear"s. "Well, we have a whole lot of talking to do," he continued, "a whole lot of information to exchange, especially now that it looks as if we are stuck with each other for the duration, or at least for the immediate future—and alas my immediate future is really *quite* immediate, quite circumscribed, as you will soon find out when we converse—so let's—" He stopped talking abruptly, bent forward, and was racked by a coughing fit so severe that I went over to him and thumped his back gently until, snorting and gasping and dribbling, he writhed back heavily in his chair and lay there breathing stertorously for some minutes. Then, in a guttural whisper, "Thank you, my dear." And louder, after he recovered, "Perhaps I should put on my mask—it's the air, I'm sure it's the filthy air, that sets off my coughing—but if I put on the mask it would be hard to talk, or at least for you to hear what I say—so let's just talk briefly for a few minutes longer, then I'll put on the mask, thank Heavens I have a whole box of them—you should put one on too, especially when you go outside." His voice had strengthened slightly. "But I want to know all about you too, my dear. We shouldn't be strangers, should we? having been neighbors for ten years. But we are. Strangers, I mean. Have you ever wondered why? So I want your answers to my questions, and I'll answer any questions that you want to ask *me*. And I'd like you to read my book and give me your honest comments on it, especially on the penultimate chapter. Do you accept?" Well, did I have any real choice? Apart from the fact that he is a retired prof, with a highly developed sense of superiority and importance, like a few I've had to deal with in the Library, or is that a mean comment? So I nodded Yes, all right. "Good. But let's first dispatch the cat issue. 'Mr Death' you call him, I believe?" "Oh—yes, but how did you know that? I never—" "Your Father mentioned it once or twice, he was amused at your calling it that. I just called it 'Tomcat'. It adopted me two years ago, just appeared at my door, and I was silly enough to feed it—until your Mother took over, at which point I decided it was merely an ungrateful swine and so I abandoned it completely to her." "But Mum would never have fed him, he killed every bird he could catch that came to Mum's bird-feeder, she hated him—and when I called him 'Mr Death' she laughed and said 'Well, I've been calling him 'Mr McGregor'. —But, yes, that's exactly who he is, Mr Death'. She would never have fed him—" "Oh yes, she did, my dear, she most certainly did. I assumed at first that she was trying to bribe him away from consuming her birds, the ones she insisted on feeding. But there's a lot you don't know about your Mother, and your

Father, and about me too, all three of us, and I think it's time—beyond time, actually—that you learned at least some of the truth, my dear. Since we have been so unexpectedly thrown together. After you appeared and disappeared yesterday, I tried to think again, long and hard, about many things, while sitting here through the night trying to get some sleep. There's nothing like pain to provoke thought—and then make it hard to think—is there? A bit like booze and sex. You must have noticed that things are rarely just what they seem to be in human affairs, and of course we can never know the whole truth anyway—but you seem to be as totally ignorant, my dear, of our complicated relations, your Father's and Mother's and mine, as they planned for you to be. Now I think it's time for me to level with you, as they say. If your parents were still alive, I'm sure they would agree. Indeed, I think they intended to tell you all about it long before now. Well, anyway, my book reveals it all, the whole saga. It's my Confession! Read the relevant chapter—take the whole lot, that whole pile of paper, with you when and if you decide to return to the Library later, I'm sick of it, and I think the printer's defunct now—you can read it there, and then we can talk about it later—though you are of course very welcome to stay here with me tonight, if you wish, and of course your own house is available to you. It appears that you have a choice of accommodation, my dear—out of three different homes! However, to finish about the cat—I'm so easily distracted these days. Once your Mother stopped feeding the birds, it was deprived of its favourite food, and soon I noticed her, when you and Barry weren't around, surreptitiously feeding it, and even petting it. No wonder it's been skulking about behind your house hoping for food—and why do you think that plastic table is there, on your deck just outside the kitchen window? Do you believe me now? Remember too that Julie, your Mother, was a most kind-hearted, sympathetic and sentimental woman—wasn't she?" I didn't reply—I'd have had to agree, though with some concealed reservations, if I'd replied, and I wasn't ready to do that yet. In fact, I felt anxious to be free of him. Some of what he'd been saying had puzzled and disturbed me.

I remained with Dr Bowman until early afternoon today, mainly doing some tidying and cleaning in his basement. He had drawn my attention to the unpleasant smell I'd noticed and tried to ignore—"My dear, the air is getting so insalubrious in this house, you must have noticed? in the washroom down here, and even worse upstairs, where I relieve myself at night. Do you think you could—?" I could, and did, carting buckets of what Mum always called Number One and Number Two outside and burying it all behind his garage. Fortunately, there were several buckets of water still available upstairs—probably Dad again, I thought, and wondered briefly why he'd done so much for Dr Bowman—and now here I am doing things in his place. When I'd finished, and squirted around some air-freshener I found in the upstairs washroom, I returned to the Library and sat here, at Dad's desk in the Librarian's Office, writing about my morning, and thinking about it. Dr Bowman had spoken nothing more of any importance, after surprising me with his story about Mum's relationship with Mr Death—I think he was in some pain by then, and also feeling very tired. Before he put on his white face-mask—with shaking hands, I noticed—he asked me to give him a glass of water, and swallowed, with a grimace, a handful of pills from a plastic medication-holder on the floor beside him. Then he gestured towards his CD player, obviously wanting me to choose a CD from among his set of 'favourites' beside it. I chose the Schubert 'Quintet in C', and we sat listening to it, so gloriously beautiful, so nobly sad, with that gentle, heartbreakingly simple slow movement—all the lovelier to me after my many days and nights of silence, silence, silence, and more silence. Before the Quintet ended, Dr Bowman was asleep, snoring softly, his mouth fallen open. Since his face was turned in my direction, I was able to study its features closely—the severe clench of his thin lips, the strong narrow prominent nose slightly tilted to the right, high cheekbones shadowing hollow cheeks, newly unkempt beard and moustache, heavy dark eyebrows above his closed blue eyes, lined broad forehead with a small scar high on the left side, thick sweep of greying hair—a handsome face, but its dominant expression, frown and downturned mouth, implying powerful negative emotions—sadness, impatience, disappointment—? And he is clearly a sick man. His face reminds me very much of Dad—Dad's face similarly turned towards me when he was dying in hospital, eyes closed, his expression one of suffering resignation. I switched off the machine quietly, replaced the CD, wrote a short note "Back this afternoon," and left it on the low table beside him, safely distant from the flickering candle—then picked up the pile of paper composing his 'book', climbed the stairs out of the basement, and went across to the Library—which, surrounded by a soft brown nimbus as I approached it, looked like a grey whale stranded, stranded and dying.

After a lunch of soup and crackers, I set the pages of Dr Bowman's 'book' in front of me on the desk, beside the Russell tome, and started to read. It was entitled, perhaps tentatively, "Coming and Going," subtitled "Where From? Where To? Notes on a Disappointed Life," and was obviously an auto-biography or memoir. Its preface begins—I'm copying it out here, "How will I be remembered? Mainly as the author of four 'influential works of criticism,' one on James Joyce's *Dubliners*, another on D.H. Lawrence's novels and short stories, a third on South African literature, the most recent on the English Liter-ature of the two World Wars; and of many critical articles and reviews? Or perhaps I should rather ask, 'Will I be remembered at all?' For most of us are remembered by only a few fellow mortals, family and friends, for the brief period until they too die. Some of us are remembered for a while longer because we have left behind some significant accomplishment, acknowledged and recorded, which carries our names forward. And a few of us—like Shakespeare, Beethoven, Michelangelo—are remembered generation after generation, as appreciation and admiration for their legacy endures, expands, and becomes traditional. Of course I do not belong in their elevated company, and will no doubt deserve to be quickly forgotten. Yet even memory of the greatest men and women must eventually end. The earth itself must eventually end. Indeed, as I write, that end may well be very near. So why am I writing these words at all? Are they merely addenda, like the snot that Stephen Dedalus placed on a rock as he wandered along the Irish strand? If they are published in any form, if they find any readers—which appears more than unlikely—why should anyone care about a boring narrative focused on one failed life? I have no answer, other than to observe that in my childhood I began what became a habit: the fascinated observation of human behaviour, searching always for the truth; and this led me to seek insight into origins and causes, into what one might call the nature of human reality. It also led me to Literature, and especially Poetry. Virginia Woolf, who believed that human experience is essentially composed of random atoms, also believed that those atoms may cohere to form patterns, and sometimes spark into what she called 'moments of being', what James Joyce called 'epiphanies', which define our actuality, who we are. 'Somewhere, everywhere, now hidden, now apparent in whatever is written down, is the form of a human being,' she wrote once. 'If we seek to know him, are we idly occupied?' In the following pages, I am seeking the form of this particular human being: the form of myself, writer of these words, I who am an individual and yet also representative of all humanity. I cannot answer Virginia Woolf's question, which is anyway rhetorical; I can only repeat it. Yet each one of us human beings, during our all-too-short journey from birth to death, from beginning to end, is essentially miraculous, and worthy of respectful contemplation. None of us is boring or negligible. Yes, we are each of us composed of similar atoms in similar patterns, but each of us is open to epiphanies: the whole of creation, in its infinity of individual trees, water, stars and other radiant beings, offers us this insight; each of us, in the varied and changing actuality of his existence, is simultaneously both like every other human throughout time, and imperatively different, diverse, unique. What to make of this paradox? We can only wonder at the nature of reality, admire it, and above all rejoice in it." At this point I put the typescript aside, thinking "Words, words, words, words." Dr Bowman's style struck me as rather overwrought and verbose, sometimes repetitive, the content pompously didactic and egotistical. Yet I was aware of some continuity, or at least connection, with what Elise and I had drawn from our encounter with the early Greek philosophers. Perhaps for that reason I was reluctant to read any further for the moment, feeling a need to meditate on what I had read, in a more patient and thoughtful frame of mind. So I decided to copy out the whole passage, as I have just done, to try to absorb it. I was tempted to turn to the penultimate chapter, the one to which Dr Bowman had particularly requested my response—but was stopped by a foreboding that seemed to be connected with the hints he had dropped about my parents, and his account of Mum's relationship with Mr Death. To smother that disquiet through activity, however random, I am now going up to the fifth floor to replace more books on the shelves, and then after five o'clock I'll go across to Dr Bowman's house as promised.

I found him listening to a CD, with a glass of wine in his hand. "Do you know this? Karl Jenkins's *Requiem*, a fairly recent discovery of mine—the fierce movement just ending is the second, his 'Dies Irae', and now the third one, such a contrast, so calm, so gentle— The words you are hearing are an ancient Japanese haiku, a 'death-song'—'The snow of yesterday that fell like cherry-blossoms is water once again'. Barry told me you write poetry—I want you to read me some of your poems. I do mean that, my dear, so don't forget! Get yourself a glass from the cupboard behind you, and join me in quaffing one of the last three bottles of wine in my cellar." "I don't really drink—" I started. "Of course you do—you're here with me now, and I insist that my companion drinks with me, how can I drink if you don't?" So I sat down opposite him with a half-filled glass of red wine. "Good!" he said, sounding quite ebullient, rejuvenated. Was he also mildly drunk, I wondered? "You know what day it is, don't you? Well, I hope you do! It's Christmas Eve. Let us drink three toasts—to God, may He be pleased to save us from destruction and restore His glorious world even though we have messed it up so badly—and to each other, my dear, may we find great happiness and fulfillment in each other's company, now that He has thrown us together at last—and to the future, that whatever it brings may include more good than evil, more happiness than suffering, and bring us life out of death." He held out his glass, I clicked mine against it, and then we both drank. Afterwards, we sat listening to the rest of the *Requiem*, which I'd never heard before and found both musically weird and emotionally disturbing—in fact, to be honest, I didn't like it. When it ended, he said, "You know, in years past, before I became arrogant and lapsed into atheism, I was a Christian, and a member of our Anglican Cathedral's congregation—an ugly building outside but beautiful within, do you know it? The organist and choir provided glorious music Sunday after Sunday. 'Hark! Joy—joy—strange joy. Music showering on our upturned listening faces', those words just came into my mind—I'm quoting from it must be Rosenberg, yes Rosenberg, of course Rosenberg, greatest of the Great War Poets. I would love to have introduced you to that joy, my dear.

And especially the joy of the Christmas Eve Midnight Mass. If only we could this evening—" He paused for a brief coughing fit, and I wondered if he was weeping now, for he turned his face away from me and seemed to be breathing heavily. After a while, "I have a favour to ask, my dear, and I ask it with—well, with humble confidence in your kindness to all old men, surely we're not so irremediably evil as some feminists have argued? Stay with me. Here. Will you? Please. Stay with me tonight and tomorrow, at least—I can't bear the thought of spending Christmas on my own. I decided last night that I have been lonely too long, truly I have. I need company, and I think it may have been God's goodness to me that you arrived when you did—I was at the end of my tether, you may not have realized that. And it was perhaps a miracle that I thought myself summoned up the stairs at that moment, just in time to see you coming out of your house. I need you, my dear. I do need you. So—you will stay with me tonight and tomorrow?" His challenging gaze troubled me, the gaze of a man unused to asking favours—but also, it seemed to me, over-emphatic and disconcertingly self-dramatizing. Yet how could I refuse? I showed my reluctance by muttering "The Library—" "—can surely look after itself tonight" he interrupted. "What do you do there, anyway, that is so important, when all the students are gone, when there are no so-called readers to operate those ranks of computers?" So I nodded a reluctant acquiescence. "Good," he said softly. "Thank you. And now we'll talk, and after that we'll go upstairs, we'll eat dinner at the dining room table, and then we'll bathe each other, and we'll sleep together and keep ourselves warm, that's the plan. Oh don't worry," as he noticed my apprehensive expression, "I couldn't rape you even if I wanted to, I'm a sick man as well as an old one, as you must've noticed. ALS—have you heard of it? Amyotrophic Lateral Sclerosis— they used to call it Lou Gehrig's disease when I was a boy, when everybody in North America knew who Lou Gehrig was, a famous baseball player—in those days it seemed to be writers and sportsmen who mainly got ALS. It's a neurological disease, the nerves waste away from the extremities inwards, and in the end, usually in a few years, maybe three, you can't talk or eat, and eventually you can't breathe. Still no cure, just pills to reduce the pain and discomfort. So you see what a joyful prospect lies before me. I was diagnosed last year, after I'd had a few falls—now I can hardly manage to climb stairs at all, but I know you'll help me tonight. That's one reason I've been living here in the basement, where I've got most of what I need all on this one level—probably also it's the reason why I started writing my memoir in earnest three months ago—my final book, I wanted to finish it, nothing concentrates the mind so much as the prospect of imminent death—Dr Johnson. But enough of that! —I just thought you ought to know, before we converse on more important topics. But I didn't want to tell you about my ALS before you agreed to spend Christmas with me, that would have seemed like blackmail. I wanted you to agree freely, not because you feel sorry for me, if you do—but of course you don't, you shouldn't, that would be insulting, my dear. I've had a long and privileged life, and so very many have died young, far too young."

After we had finished our wine in silence, Dr Bowman suddenly stirred and, as he handed me his empty glass to place on the table, exclaimed "Well, now let's go up and enjoy our Christmas Eve feast." I helped him rise from the armchair, and then he clung to me as we slowly climbed the stairs to the first floor. "The dining room table, please, my dear," he wheezed, after we paused so he could catch his breath. "I'll sit at the far end. Then if you could lay the table, the cloth and cutlery and crockery are in the kitchen drawers and I'll tell you where to find cans of soup and turkey and vegetables and fruit—and we'll need two more glasses so we can quaff the bottle of white South African wine, alas not chilled, that you'll find in one of the kitchen cupboards." While I followed his instructions, he continued: "Did you know it was Barry who was entirely responsible for my store of food? —in fact, he built it up with contributions when he brought home his own provisions, all the time urging me to prepare for the disaster to come—I was sceptical at first, he was showing obvious signs of dementia by then—but he was so insistent that it was hard to resist, and by the time I followed his example in earnest, widespread panic-buying was beginning—and he was right, of course, about the disaster. He was right about many things, your Father. And wrong about a few. Shall I say Grace? We thank you, dear God, for this plenty when so many lack food and drink, and we thank you for our continuing life when so many have died." As I opened the first cans, he commented, "It's a pity we didn't also think, Barry and I, about buying small kerosene stoves, like the ones we used in picnics years ago, surely you can still get those? Then we could have warmed our food tonight and enjoyed it much more, I'm getting so tired of cold food, and you must be tired of it too. Now, before we eat—a toast to Barry and Julie, your parents, and my friends, who gave both of us love and sustenance." I echoed him, with some puzzlement, as we raised our glasses, "To Mum and Dad," adding under my breath "and Elise and Thumper." After that there was silence until we finished our soup, then Dr Bowman cleared his throat. "And now let me start telling you about myself and your parents. I won't go into detail, you'll find that in my book when you read it, and I'll also save time and effort by being plain and even abrupt. About myself first. I was born in August 1955, the youngest of three sons, in a remote mission hospital in South Africa, where my father was a United Church missionary. Just before I turned seven, my parents returned to Canada, and we settled for a few years in Vancouver, except for my eldest brother, who opted to stay in Africa. At thirteen I discovered that I was gay, I'm sure that will be no surprise to you? Actually, I should perhaps say I was bisexual—but none of the sex-labels are much use, in my view. Certainly, by the time I was at university studying English and music, I was sexually active, even promiscuous, attracting the attentions of several older men, including my music professor—I was a pretty boy in those days, real 'eye-candy', as the expression went. But I was also a serious student, with a love of literature, and ambitions to do research and teach at university level, so I avoided the drugs-and-party scene, and, after a first-class B.A. and with a major scholarship, I came to this University as a graduate student in September 1977. Eventually I was forced to focus on Canadian and what was then called Commonwealth literature, so as to get a teaching job as a lecturer in Manitoba, where I got my Ph.D. a couple of years later—but my great love was First and Second World War poetry, I'll read you some later, we'll both read some of our favourite poems to each other, and your own poetry too—so when I found out that there was a research collection of war literature here, I applied and was accepted into the English Department's M.A. program. Sorry this is taking so long, and I'm leaving out a lot, but I hope it's useful background. To what? To my relationship with your Father and Mother, mainly. That started when my M.A. thesis supervisor arranged for me to meet Barry, since, as you probably know, apart from being University Librarian, he was teaching a course in modern European history and had published articles on the Second World War that would be useful for the historical component of my research into Keith Douglas, a Second War poet who was killed on the beaches of Normandy in June 1944 and is still alas much less known and appreciated than Wilfred Owen and all the other major First War poets. Meeting Barry, in his University Librarian's Office, was one of the really memorable experiences of my life. He was in his mid-thirties, newly appointed, just eleven years older than me, if I remember rightly—my supervisor had told me that he was a high-flyer, recently recruited from Scotland's National Library to re-organize and re-energize this Library, but no one had told me he was such a gorgeous charismatic man, tall and slim with dark, deep-set blue eyes and a beautiful low sexy voice, I always love that! We spent most of that hour talking about ourselves—he told me that his interest in war history had been sparked, you know this of course, by his father's heroism in the Second War, and subsequent mental suffering and early death as a result of horrific experiences he could neither forget nor talk about. And Barry told me his father had actually known Keith Douglas, not in the War but before it, as a fellow undergraduate at Merton College, Oxford, where they were both tutored by Edmund Blunden. After that initial occasion, we met often, Barry and I, usually in the late afternoon, to drink and talk, in a corner of the Faculty Club at first, and later in his home office. We quickly became close friends, and eventually more than friends. He introduced me to Julie of course, and she too became a friend—she would often invite me to 'stay for a wee supper' and sometimes, if Barry was detained at board or committee meetings, she and I would sit and talk and drink sherry, she loved hearing my childhood memories of South Africa and she would tell me about *her* childhood in Stirling. This went on for several months, I even had Christmas with them that year because my parents were in Nigeria and my brother Neil was in some skiing competition at Whistler—but then Julie had to fly back to Edinburgh in the fall of 1979, her father was ill, and— Let me be brief now, Barry and I found ourselves one evening in his living room, both a little drunk, and he suddenly said 'Come here, Ben, I need to—' and hugged me tight and kissed me, we were both aroused, and went upstairs and spent the night in his bed. If you are shocked, my dear, I might say that he was obviously very inexperienced, but I'm sure we both enjoyed ourselves—and continued to do so after Julie's return—in various locations, including the University Librarian's Office. Of course we talked often and intensely about our situation—he felt very guilty about deceiving Julie, and especially it troubled him that he and she were having sex together less frequently. Before that Christmas, he told me he had decided he must tell her that he thought he was gay. I had argued, but not forcefully, against that—it was *his* decision, but I feared it might end the marriage—it didn't, and that was mainly because Julie behaved with admirable sense and sensibility. I felt a bit guilty when I first encountered her after she returned, a week before Christmas, but she seemed just the same as ever, welcoming and chatty, in fact even more than before. So it was a very happy Christmas and then our lives ran on, quite smoothly—but my exams and viva were inevitably approaching, and after that I would be moving on and away. Barry and I were, I can only say it like this, my dear—we were very deeply in love, I have never loved another man as I loved him, and never could—though I have had several relationships since then, some lasting over a year, and the one with Piet, in Cape Town, lasted seven years and would have lasted— But I didn't, being young and foolish, understand until later the depth of our love, Barry's and mine, especially in those glorious years, 1979 and 1980. So. That's the story, my dear. What do you— Do you have any comments? Ask me any questions you like, I promise to answer them as honestly as I can."

Even with my 'total recall', I can't be sure that I have transcribed Ben's 'story' fully and accurately, though I've tried to. He ordered me during our Christmas Eve dinner to stop calling him 'Dr Bowman' and I am trying to get used to 'Ben'. I know, of course, Dad quite often said it, that history is not as factual as even a historian might hope and intend—and he insisted that biography should be called 'fiction with a few facts', "it should be catalogued under 'Fiction' actually." Anyway, as I say, I'm trying to write down, record, what I can as honestly as possible—there aren't many blank pages left in this notebook, and among other challenges is the fact that there never seems to be sufficient time for recording what has happened. I am writing this now on the afternoon of the day after Christmas—Boxing Day—back in the University Librarian's Office, after sleeping last night in my old bed at home. Ben made me promise to return to his house this evening, and I still have much to write—and I must also think out what I should do in the immediate future. I think I know what he wants from me—he hasn't said what that is, but I can guess, and I want to be prepared—it will come soon and I know it'll be hard to say 'No' to him. Now, in the last few pages of this notebook, I must try to summarize what else happened yesterday. After our Christmas Eve dinner, and Ben's speech, he sat in silence while I tidied up. Then I helped him to an armchair in his living room, and sat on the couch, near him. "You don't say anything, my dear. Why not? Have I hurt you, should I have stayed silent? I thought you should know—" "Yes," I answered him after a moment, "you were right to tell me, I'm glad to know what you told me—it doesn't change anything, at least not damagingly, I loved my parents and I still love them. But—" "What? But what?" "Well, it leaves some questions dangling, like why did they always say quite negative things about *you* after you moved into this house ten years ago, why did they seem to want to discourage me from getting to know or even talk to you, why didn't they introduce us, or ever mention that they had known you for so many years? Surely— And yet you were in close contact with them—you said he urged you to prepare for The End, and so on, why didn't I know about any of that? I don't understand. Why?" His silence made me wonder if I'd annoyed him, but then he said "So let me explain, my dear, how it was that I returned here, and bought this house next door to yours." He coughed, cleared his throat. "I was teaching at the University of Cape Town just before that, when Piet, my beloved partner of seven years, died of AIDS—a dreadful time, a truly dreadful time. Barry and I had kept in quite frequent touch over the years, and so I e-mailed him with the news of Piet's death, no doubt dwelling on my pain and despair—but he was always very perceptive and would have known how I was feeling anyway. He replied, 'Why don't you come back here? you belong here—Julie and I would love that, and by coincidence the house beside us is coming up for sale'—and later he explained that its owner was an old friend—perhaps they had even been lovers, something he said later made me wonder about that. Anyway, Barry was the executor of his will, the owner's will. So that's how I came back—I took early retirement from the University of Cape Town, and then I used most of my savings for a mortgage to buy this house. What did I have in my mind? Well, my earlier interest in war literature had revived, and I had begun a critical book on it, so the Library's war literature collection was again an attraction. But more importantly, Barry's e-mails had been full of affectionate comments, so perhaps I was also hoping that we could renew and deepen our earlier relationship—perhaps we were *both* hoping that—and he was certainly friendly enough after my return here, but I soon realized that anything like our first relationship wouldn't happen—for various reasons, one being Julie, another being you and your sister, you were both at home then. Almost as soon as I settled in, and invited Barry and Julie and other neighbours round, she took the opportunity to corner me in the kitchen and instruct me on the behavior she expected—no contact with you being the major requirement. 'He has been working in the Library for many years, that's where he is right now in fact, and he seems to be extremely happy there. Barry and I were very worried about him, when he was in his teens, especially when he insisted on dropping out of high school, after they said he was autistic. So now we don't want his life disturbed in any way.' Did she think I would 'interfere' with you sexually, I wondered angrily, when I had actually done my best to help years earlier? But I kept the peace—and during the years since then I have also wondered if that was a mistake, staying silent— So often I would see you walking to and from the Library, from your house to the Library and back again, always alone, always silent, head down. We could have got together and enjoyed conversations about literature, and, once I was teaching again, in the English Department—they needed someone to teach post-colonial literature and supervise some graduate research, and got me cheap as I was right here and only too anxious for employment—then I could have helped you in studying for a degree in English literature or at least taking some extracurricular courses that you might have enjoyed. —But Barry was adamant, he told me that yes, you were extremely sensitive, and intelligent, just as Julie had told me—and loved reading, as well as writing poetry and short stories—and of course, he said, Julie was right to try to protect you from strain, from the destructive effects of any pressure. Barry and I would get together for occasional decorous drinks or lunches in the Faculty Club, and sometimes, for something to say, probably, as our relationship weakened and our conversation dwindled, he would give me some information about you. —I hardly ever saw Julie, who, as you know, was at that time wrapped up in your sister and her diabetes, and then later the marriage, and visiting her in the States. So now you know why our paths never crossed in all these years—though once or twice we almost bumped into each other on the way to or from the University, as you must remember, and of course we would say hullo and smile stiffly at each other. You were in your early thirties—and I would wonder if you were enjoying any of the great fundamental pleasures that life offers, especially love, friendship, sex." I didn't respond to his implied question, and instead asked, "What did you mean when you said you had 'done your best to help years earlier'?" "Oh. Oh, my dear, I wonder if it's worth discussing that episode now, it was so long ago, over twenty-five years ago, my memory of it is a bit hazy—I remember you were thirteen, the summer of 1994, I think it was. You wouldn't have known me, or even that I existed. I had been away since 1980, first in Manitoba, then in the UK and Africa, and I came back here for a few weeks that summer, and stayed with one of the friends of my graduate-student days—hoping of course that Barry and I could get together. But instead he asked me to look after his brother-in-law, your uncle Andrew—Barry had booked him into a hotel downtown, he was a mess, a drug addict I thought—apparently he'd made a nuisance of himself when he was a guest in your house, he'd interfered with you in some way, Barry said, and he also said that even Julie was angry and disgusted with him. So I tried to befriend him, as Barry had requested, and took him to Niagara Falls, showed him around Toronto, and so on—he had another week in Canada before returning to Singapore, where he was teaching English, and where, as I'm sure you know, he was arrested for pedophile activities a year later and committed suicide in prison there." No, I didn't know that, and I didn't want to know that. It was bad enough to find myself raging inwardly, as I recalled helplessly, compulsively, obsessively, Uncle Andrew coming into my bedroom—Mum and Dad were out that evening, at meetings, the house was silent—he pushed me back onto my bed and pulled down my jeans.

No more space, almost! Only one page left, as you see. Yet I still have a lot to record about Christmas Eve and Christmas Day, and will try to do that tomorrow in the notebook that I have fortunately found in Dad's 'secret place'—after I had looked unsuccessfully for a notebook both at home and in the Library. It's Dad's notebook, of course, though only the first few pages were covered with his writing. Before I found it, it seemed as if he was standing beside me and telling me where to look for it— I was sitting here, at his desk in the University Librarian's Office, and suddenly I remembered the first time I was ever in this room—I must have been six or seven, and Dad, he was showing me where he worked—but once we came into this wide high-ceilinged room, I was over-awed, stricken into silence, so he tried to entertain and relax me by saying "Did you know there's a secret place in my desk? Yes, there is, and I bet you can't find it!"—and he lifted me up and sat me in his big revolving chair, and I pulled open all the drawers on the right and the left, now filled with Dr Goode's stuff—and eventually I discovered the slim drawer concealed right in the centre of the desk, immediately under where I am writing these words—I don't remember what was in the drawer then, all those years ago, but today it contained only a large black-covered notebook. Thanks, Dad!

IV

3.vii.1978   My first day in this Office! A few days ago, the University President welcomed me effusively over the telephone, & soon I am to be put on show in the Senate. It is all quite overwhelming! I fear that my task here may well be overwhelming too: my predecessor has left me a memo to the effect that this Library has been starved of funds for many years, so that purchasing of books & magazines has been severely diminished; & it is quite evident that the building itself is in need of renovation. In addition, the Provost informed me, in strict confidence, that my predecessor had resigned owing to some scandal (he gave no details & I asked for none); then he went on to hint that I had been appointed because I come from afar, &, though unusually young for the position, was "exceptionally well-recommended in my field as effective but discreet"! So, major challenges are already emerging, with more to follow, inevitably. I will certainly need to be both circumspect & forceful. So let me get started! I'm relieved that J. is pleased with the house, which is conveniently close to the campus & my daily work; also so much bigger than we anticipated: "It needs children!" she exclaimed this morning.

26.xii.1978   Our first Christmas in Canada. I think we have settled quite well, though J. said yesterday, "Don't you think it might have been a mistake to come here?" But then she has been depressed by the sudden death of her mother in Stirling last month, & feels deeply the lack of family & close friends, while I have been too busy even to notice. Mea culpa! May 1979 be a happy & successful year for us both.

3.x.1979   I am still in shock! I had no idea, no idea at all, that one man could love another as I do B.! I mean sexually as well as in every other way. He is my alpha and omega, he is my Life! I struggle not to think of him every moment of every day, I dream about him every night, I long to be with him even in the midst of chairing an important meeting. Sometimes my love for him is so distracting that it seems as much a curse as a blessing; but whenever I can be with him, if only for a few minutes, Oh then it is ecstasy, sheer ecstasy! I have only one real worry: should I tell J. and if so when?

22.viii.1980   B. left today. How can I survive this? I feel bereft, utterly bereft. We promised each other to keep in daily contact, by telephone as well as mail, & to find ways to be together as often as possible.

29.xii.1980   My son born today! I was there! He emerged into the world blind but smiling.

30.viii.1983   Delirious three-week holiday with B. in Cape Breton; which seems to be much more Scottish than Scotland! J. & P. in Stirling with her father & family. B. & I have decided that we must go on holiday together every summer!

4.vi.1992   J. wants to adopt a daughter: says she has always longed for one. Of course I agreed, & am enquiring about the process. Could be helpful for P. to have a little sister too: he needs companions: would encourage him to be more sociable & self-confident.

13.viii.1994   B. here for two weeks but alas no opportunity to be with him—because of crisis caused by bloody Andrew— accused by P. of sexually abusing him, A. denied it, J. very upset, "her little brother, how could I possibly think he would do such a thing?" etc., so I tried to calm everything down &

keep the peace—arranged for A. to be in a hotel downtown for his final week—B. agreed to keep him occupied till he left yesterday—but meant I hardly saw B. at all. Why doesn't he come back more often—or could we meet at a conference next summer perhaps?

21.xi.1994   What a joy! Our little seven-year-old daughter with her sunny, extrovert temperament is a wonderfully positive addition to our family. We all love her.

5.vi.1998   Arranged for P. to work in the Library, re-shelving books etc.—temporary job, as I told J., but he seems to love books even more than I do, & writes poetry though he won't let me see it—the job may do him good, give him encouragement & draw him out—all that autism & ADD speculation demoralized him I think—he's shy, as I was at his age—needs self-confidence, & then he'll blossom, I know he will!

18.vii.2009   F.'s wedding. She looked radiantly lovely, and felt so fragile as she leaned on my arm on the way into the church.

4.xi.2009   B. arrived—looked haggard, exhausted. Said I looked pale & tired too! Well, we have both recently endured major loss, & almost concurrently—is that a positive omen for a renewal of our old relationship? Both of us have had other lovers, but now we can be together again at last. Showed him over R.'s house & he decided immediately to take it, will move in tomorrow—J. arrived just as we were having a drink, said she was exhausted after a long contentious interview with a client, must get to bed—both she & B. seemed a bit shy, nervous of each other: only natural after so many years.

20.vii.2010   Elected President of the Association: some recognition at last for all my work as University Librarian—

compensates a little for the hostile criticism I endure here, especially behind my back—they wanted international eminence but didn't want to pay for it—further cutbacks in the Library budget—& no further acquisitions of major papers permitted, even for the War and Peace Collection—money unavailable for that, only for more & more huge buildings (to be named after them, of course).

19.ix.2010   They want me to retire next year, when I turn 65, the old required age for retirement. "An excellent retirement package," the VP informed me, but that cannot disguise the fact that I am being pushed. No doubt they have some young turk in view who will be expected to remedy his predecessor's failings, as I was once employed to do; & no doubt I should move aside with dignity; but the hurt is deep. Oh, if I could be with B. again, & as we once were! He seems distant, cold, whenever we meet now.

29.v.2011   My retirement party—insincere commendations from Goode & others—& weak jokes—I smiled & said my own insincere piece—well, perhaps I am being unfair to both my successor & myself—retirement is as inevitable as death and taxes—old age, too, of course, & I am increasingly aware of how my memory fails, how words fall through the cracks of my mind and are lost forever—as I am lost—or fear I am—a failure professionally and personally—& a failure as husband, father, lover.

Dad's Fragments. I was deeply moved by them on first reading, and wept again as I thought about them, and that's all I can say about them at the moment. As I sit at his desk, here exactly where he sat day after day, during all the years of his career as University Librarian, from 1978 to his retirement in 2011, thirty-three years in all, I feel as if he is very near, inside me as well as outside—that if time could be peeled back, he is sitting here at this desk writing his words, as I am sitting here writing *my* words—that in some strange way we exist both separately and together. No, I can't explain it any better! We are, and are not. What I must do now is summarize the rest of our time together, Ben and I, through Christmas Eve and Christmas Day. I have visited Ben a couple of times since then, and eaten meals with him, after taking over another lot of cans and bottles of water from Dad's store. Nothing notable to report following those occasions—in fact, since Christmas Day we have both been quiet, hardly any conversation, and he has sometimes been restless and irascible—mainly, I think because of increasing physical discomfort. But also there is tension between us. We can't continue much longer like this. At the same time there has been no notable external change, except one—and the weather, if you can call it that, continues gloomily grey, and the temperature, though a bit cooler, is still well above freezing—warmer even than last winter, I think—maybe because of the constant heavy cloud cover. No sun! And no snow. And no rain, for so long—the soil dry, dry, and brown— the grass too, no lawns left around the Library, just dry brown cracked clay, and dust when the wind blows. No sunlight! Probably both of us, Ben and I, are beginning to suffer from Vitamin D deficiency, we both have unnaturally pale skin—but no sign of the Brown Death for us so far! —However, I don't feel well, in fact I feel sicker and weaker by the day, coughing more often and more rackingly, if one can say that! and both of us are suffering from occasional sharp attacks of diarrhea, perhaps caused by our diet. I have to fight off depression more and more—but regular re-shelving of books helps me, by generating gentle continuous focused activity, and so distracting me from some at least of my blackest thoughts— soon I should have all the outstanding returned books re- shelved, and that will be satisfying.

The one notable change? Yesterday morning I went across to our house to feed Mr Death, as I have been doing every day, but this time there was no sign of him, to my surprise—I pushed sardines and water out the back door, and waited for him to leap up into view from underneath the deck. When he didn't, some intuition prompted me go out into the yard and towards the edge of the ravine—but even before I got there, I saw it, a small pile of white bones and the remnants of a black pelt. But who or what had killed him? Although I did feel sad and almost a sense of loss, it was the question of the perpetrator or perpetrators that made me look around nervously, and down into the ravine. When I went across to Ben's house and down into his basement, to serve and join him in another of our cold, monotonous and increasingly repellent meals, and broke the silence by informing him about his cat's fate, he smiled faintly and chanted softly "'Death, thou shalt be no more, Death, thou shalt die,'" the final line of one of Donne's Holy Sonnets. "But what do you think did it?" I asked Ben. "That's what troubles me. I haven't seen any predator, any animal at all, not when I walked into the centre of Westgreen, and not when I've walked to and from the Library, which I have been doing several times a day, as you know." "How about a vampire or zombie? —Oh, I'm just joking of course, my dear" when he saw how I reacted— not that I would actually credit a vampire as Mr Death's murderer, of course, but it was an unwelcome reminder of *The Last Man on Earth,* and especially of its tragic conclusion—I'd casually mentioned the movie to Ben at some point. "I've been intending to tell you, my dear," he continued, "that during the night of Christmas Day, which you remember you spent in your house, I woke up thinking I had heard a sound, and I needed a pee, so I dragged myself to the bathroom, and when I looked out the window I saw movements, in fact what might have been two animals—just shadows skulking in the darkness, but I could see what looked like flashes of pale green eyes, and then they were gone. There could be raccoons around still, and *they* are certainly capable of killing a cat. But what I thought is that the ones I saw looked more like coyotes—pale brown fur, I think, and just loping in silence like wolves, and you know how coyotes have invaded cities and suburbs more and more over the years, to forage for food. And, you must also know, they will attack and kill human beings if they're starving, and they hunt in packs, don't they? So you should take great care, especially walking to the Library at night." When I went back to our house, before going over to the Library, I was careful to take the untouched sardines and water back into the kitchen, to avoid attracting raccoons, coyotes, or any other predators that may be haunting the neighborhood—maybe they can still find food, in garbage cans and backyards, but when the supply is exhausted, what then? I took out Dad's shovel for, I hoped, the last time, and buried Mr Death's pathetic remains in a very shallow grave that I dug beside Mum's, on the side opposite to Thumper's—an angel on one side, a devil on the other, I thought sardonically—two companions on her journey, one white, one black, both of them animals whom she loved—well, she had petted Thumper and fed Mr Death, so surely they both loved *her.*

But Ben and I—what else is worth recording of our Christmas festivities? After the Christmas Eve dinner, he said it was imperative, if we were to sleep together—as he had decided we would, without of course consulting me—that we should sponge-bathe each other first. "As you've seen, I still have four buckets of water in the bathroom," he announced, "one should be sufficient if we are careful." "But it'll be freezing cold, it'll kill us," I complained, "and you're in no condition—" "Oh, my dear, where is your pioneering Canadian spirit? And I can assure you that you do stink, we both stink. And think how noble in form, as well as pure in spirit, you will be afterwards. You will be excessively grateful to me—cleanliness is next to godliness,

I'm sure your Mother told you that?" So, in candlelight, we sponge-bathed each other, and in fact the whole 'cleanliness' experience did have a bracingly positive effect, emotionally as well as physically—we laughed with and at each other, a sort of wild nervous giggling, while, standing in the bath, we sponged icy water onto each other's naked bodies, then soaped each other, sponged again, and finally towelled each other dry—and throughout the process were insanely ebullient. Then we staggered to Ben's bedroom, he clinging to me, and threw ourselves under several blankets on his king-sized bed, and warmed up our shivering bodies, and continued our boyish silliness for a while longer, tickling each other, and giggling—"like a couple of schoolgirls", Mum would have said—until Ben was afflicted by a coughing fit and gasped "Pax, pax, my dear—pax," and after that we settled for sleep, lying on our sides, I behind Ben in the 'spoon' position—and we slept a warm deep sleep, oh how deeply we slept! right through the night and late into Christmas morning. There was nothing at all sexual in our romping, or sponging, or when we were in bed together—which was just as well, considering the event which later brought division between us.

On Christmas Day, our 'Celebratory Poetry Reading', another of Ben's projects! Having consumed a breakfast of fruit and cookies, we settled ourselves amicably, side by side on the living room sofa, sharing a blanket flung over our knees and chests—and read aloud, alternately, a series of poems that we each selected from the anthology I had brought down, at his instruction, from Ben's office. As I handed the book to him, he ordered "In the top kitchen cupboard, you'll find an unopened bottle of Scotch, that noble lubrication of your ancestry—bring it here with two glasses, and pour us both a sufficient libation to honor the occasion," and soon I found myself sipping whisky for the first time in my life, at first cautiously, and then appreciating its sharply warming effect and distinctive mellow taste.

Ben had raised his glass—"Let us drink to the Glory of Words, the Greatness of Literature, the Joy of Poetry. And now, sir, choose your weapons for the royal joust—we shall begin with our favourites of the moment, of this very moment. And I shall go first, since I am older than you, my dear"—by some twenty-five years, I thought—and at that very moment some fragments began to cohere, a pattern began to form.

How can I summarize our reading? Only, in the main, with some titles and fragments—a few brief quotations from the poems, in the only text we used, Volume Two of *The Norton Anthology of English Poetry*, "once ubiquitous in modern English poetry courses," Ben had stated as I put the book into his hands, "I mean when universities still tolerated seminars in modern English poetry—I keep it as a memento of some of my most enjoyable teaching experiences, and to consult and cherish it when depressed about the state of the Academy today." So, sitting forward alternately on the sofa, with the anthology on our lap, we read aloud our selected poems. Both of us had at times to pause, clear our throats, cough, but we found sufficient voice, and applauded each other generously until mutual exhaustion ended the performance. "That was a damn good show, hey—a tribute to poets who have shown us in our time who we are and can be, poets who have plumbed the nature of our reality!" was Ben's verdict, as we slumped back together, sighing and sated. I murmured agreement, and we both contentedly emptied our glasses. That's how the occasion should have ended, in harmonious enjoyment, but no doubt we were both drunk even then, on words and rhythm, on alliteration and assonance, on images and symbols, as the whisky began to work its balefully transformative magic.

—D.H. Lawrence, "The Ship of Death"—"And death is on the air like a smell of ashes! / Ah! can't you smell it?"—"We are dying, we are dying, we are all of us dying"—"It is the end, it is oblivion"—"Ah wait, wait, for there's the dawn, / the cruel dawn of coming back to life / out of oblivion"—and finally, so beautiful, so consoling, "Swings the heart, renewed with peace." Ben's favourite of favourites. He read it warmly, lovingly.

—T.S. Eliot, "Little Gidding," fourth of *The Four Quartets*—"Midwinter spring is its own season"—"Every phrase and every sentence is an end and a beginning, / Every poem an epitaph"—"We shall not cease from exploration"—"Quick now, here, now, always." *My* favourite of favourites.

—And after that we rambled from poem to poem, passing the anthology to each other, sometimes declaiming our chosen poems fiercely, sometimes reciting them quietly, meditatively—Keith Douglas, "Vergissmeinnicht," Wilfred Owen, "Strange Meeting," Philip Larkin, "MCMXIV," W.H. Auden, "The Shield of Achilles," Isaac Rosenberg, "Dead Man's Dump," Robert Graves, "The Cool Web," W.B.Yeats, "Sailing to Byzantium," Thomas Hardy, "The Darkling Thrush"—and others that I can't recall. But I do remember my final choice, Eliot's "The Waste Land"—"These fragments I have shored against my ruins." Yes. These fragments, my ruins.

"And let us not forget our grand climax—your own poems, my dear, by urgent request and prior agreement. Please." Ben leaned back, breathing heavily, and closed his eyes. "Well, there are only two I think I can recall accurately," I said, "I haven't written poems for quite a while. This first one of these I remember composing in a state of intense emotion, when I felt surrounded by menacing destructive forces, I was sixteen. Here it is:

> "Before the axe descends
> and blood proclaims a birth,
> no beginnings and no ends
> ungreen the green of earth.
> —All's one, continuous
> as the muscled lift and sweep,
> the gradual fall upon us,
> the shining axe of sleep."

I sat back, waiting for a professorial comment from Ben, but none came. So I went on to the second poem. "This one is called 'Warnings' and it was written a few months later, maybe when I had been reading something about the continuing danger of nuclear war or some other disaster—but I don't think it's very specifically about that." I cleared my throat and recited slowly and softly:

> "Children will touch our skulls
> among the piles of dusty bones
> gently and with awe,
> wondering what this jones
> or smith saw
> that made him stare at the white sky
> and drop his jaw
> to scream or grin and die.
> —But soon again their joyful yells
> will clutch the silence when they play
> with heads of men who once were tall
> and splendidly built.
> —We played ball
> too, were often gay
> in spite of our guilt."

Silence, silence. Eventually I said "Of course when I wrote that I was using 'gay' with the basic original meaning, maybe I didn't know then about the additional meaning, the sexual one, which has now almost taken over completely, hasn't it?—'last year's words belong to last year's language', yes—'And next year's words await another voice.'" Silence again. Silence. I turned towards Ben, whose head was drooped over his chest, eyes still closed tight. After a moment he raised his head, twisted it about, sighed deeply, opened his eyes, and said loudly "More whisky! We need more whisky! Fill our glasses, my dear—we'll finish the bottle, it's the very last one—we'll drink life to the lees in honor of poetry—history and poetry. Your Father would have loved to be here." "Philosophy too," I added harshly.

I see now that my unfamiliar belligerence after Ben's speech was partly caused by a reaction to the tiring exhilaration of our reading, and to Ben's silence, which I had interpreted as negative criticism—but mostly, of course, to the whisky I'd already drunk, with its novel and intense effect on my mind and body. As I stood swaying, and pouring whisky very carefully into Ben's proffered glass, I heard myself, vehemently, and unexpectedly, snapping at him. "And don't say anything about my Father, Ben. Just don't." He sipped, blinked, then gazed up into my eyes, searchingly. "What's the matter, my dear? Why do you sound so angry suddenly?" I finished pouring whisky into my glass, then threw back my head and swigged such a searing mouthful, as I sat down beside him, that I gagged, nearly vomited, and had to struggle with a coughing fit. When I could speak again, hoarsely, "You didn't say anything about my poems, you didn't make even one comment." He smiled wryly, which may have enraged me further—then "And *you* haven't commented on my book, have you, my dear? On the chapter I asked you to read?" I was shivering with an extreme implosive fury that I had not experienced since my parents told me, a few weeks after Uncle Andrew's visit, that they were adopting a seven-year-old girl, "a sister for you, isn't that wonderful? And she'll be with us tomorrow! We'll bring her home tomorrow, she's so pretty and lively, you'll love her, we know you will, even more than your Father and I do"—a huge shock, since I hadn't heard anything about adoption for at least a year after the social worker had visited us and looked around our house with Mum, and interviewed me—and so I had concluded, with relief, that the adoption wouldn't happen.

Of course, at that time I hadn't started listening every night to Mum and Dad's bedroom conversations—I began that only after Fiona arrived.

Now Ben was gazing at me, "My dear, what is it? Are you feeling ill? Please tell me." But I could hardly hear what he was saying for the uneven banging of my heart, my stuttering lungs, aching throat, the roar in my ears—I stood up, turned, almost fell, and shouted down at him "'Your Father, your Father'—who *is* my Father? Why do you go on trying to fool me, why do you lie to me? Who *is* my Father, Ben? Tell me who my Father is. Tell me." "What do you mean?" though of course he must have known what I meant. I tried to control myself, gabbled "You told me that Dad was gay, and you and he were lovers—you told me that when you first came here, forty years ago, you were bisexual, that's what you said—you told me Mum wanted to have children—of course that's the reason they had to adopt Fiona later—you told me you and Mum would often be alone together—and—" "All right, my dear, I can see where this is going, I'm not really surprised you've put it all together, you're like your Father, perceptive, analytical—I used to tell him he should have been a detective—" "Don't say 'your Father'," I screamed, then turned away from him and started to weep, shamefully, "*you're* my Father, aren't you? That's why we both love poetry—Dad never did—and that's why we— *You're* my Father, and you abandoned me—you didn't care about me, you just—you ran away—" He leaned towards me, took my right hand to pull me down beside him, and gently put his left arm round my shoulders. "All right, my dear, all right. I'll tell you everything I know, perhaps I should have told you earlier—I'm sorry, I'm sorry for any pain I've caused. I love you." "'*Love*' me, '*love*' me!" I pulled away from him. "How can you say that? It's a hateful lie, it's *shit*. You fucked Mum, didn't you, she wanted a baby, maybe she and Dad weren't sleeping together but *you* wanted sex, she gave you what you wanted so she could get what *she* wanted, that's how—isn't it?—and Dad thought—I don't know what Dad thought—" "Well, just slow down, my dear. I'll tell you the truth, the whole truth as far as I know it, I promise—but you must calm down first. —Here, lean against me, breathe slowly and deeply, yes, like that."

Then, quietly, steadily, with occasional pauses to catch his breath, Ben told me what had happened—he told me that, one evening in March 1980, he and Mum were drinking sherry together, Dad was at a meeting, and they kissed and hugged, "I don't remember exactly how it happened, who started it, but I was a young man in my mid-twenties, and you must know that young men are randy, I could have fucked a tree at that time in my life—and also, let me admit this, I hadn't had sex with a woman, and I guess I wanted to know if I could do it, what it was like, and Julie gave me the opportunity—in fact we had sex, penetrative sex, only once or twice more, if I remember correctly, it wasn't something I really wanted, it felt strange with her—what I really wanted was to be with Barry, and I was relieved when he told me a couple of months later that Julie thought she was pregnant and wanted to go back to Scotland, while she could still travel without complications, to see her family—she was worried about her father because he had been ill and wasn't managing well as a widower. So Barry and I were alone for a while, and that was the happiest, the most intense time we ever had together—apart from a holiday in Nova Scotia during the summer of 1983—we would drive to the cottage at Lion's Head, he rented it that spring and later he bought it—and we would swim, and canoe, and walk the Bruce Trail, and make love all night. And talk! How we talked! I think we enjoyed our conversations so much, in those delirious reckless weeks up there on the Bruce Peninsula, because we were so deeply in love that we yearned to know everything about each other—but also because, even though we had so much in common, there were, you're right of course, personal differences, idiosyncrasies—he was cerebral, the Historian, the Librarian, focusing on dates and facts and analysis, while I was intuitive, a lover of music and literature, especially poetry, 'sloppy self-indulgent romantic emotion' was his phrase when he was teasing me—and how we teased each other, how we laughed and laughed! And learned from each other. Ecstasy, radiant happiness—it was idyllic. But it had to end of course. By the time I left for Manitoba, in late August, Julie was just back, and very obviously pregnant now—and she clearly didn't want to have much to do with me, in fact I could see she was subtly avoiding me, so I kept out of her way. I'm pretty sure that Barry never suspected anything, why would he? and I'm pretty sure that Julie never told him, why would she? I guess I felt some guilt, but I was a young man, the world and all its pleasures were there for the taking—I don't excuse my behavior, but it's how I was, and I wasn't unique—I didn't want to be tied-down, I was young, I was ambitious, I wanted a successful academic career. And what could I do anyway, when Julie didn't want me around? Also I guess I told myself, especially after I heard about your birth at the end of that year, that I wasn't your Father, Barry was—and he was so very proud of you, of having a son, of being a father—that I thought that it would be wrong for me to say or do anything to spoil that. I loved him very deeply, you must believe that—so, apart from sending congratulations after you were born, I didn't do anything. Even when we were talking, he and I, or writing to each other quite intimately about our lives, and mentioned the past, later on, neither of us ever referred to the events of 1980—deliberately on my side and perhaps on his too. And that's how it was, almost until I came back to live here ten years ago. By then I had been in several relationships, mostly short-term, in several different countries. Barry and I had kept in touch, loosely—but I wonder now exactly why he arranged for me to come back here—I can only surmise that he was moved by my near-collapse after Piet died, I had nursed him through AIDS—and then coincidentally this house had become available. —But Barry was always a truly kind and generous and gentle man, and not only to me—I know some people thought him severe, unsympathetic, remote, but that was shyness, he was a man to be loved and admired, and I always did love and admire him. So— Now to your question, my dear. I can't answer it! I truly can't answer it. And that must be my answer. We could have found out at any time during the past ten years, through DNA testing, if we had all four wanted that—Barry, Julie, me, and of course you—but that would have meant revealing what I've been telling you, and it was very clear to me that Barry and especially Julie would be opposed. I had slowly realized, during my first months back here, that there was some awkwardness, some tension, between Barry and Julie that perhaps also involved you and me—I could only speculate that my return might have provoked Julie to confess that she and I had had sex together before you were born, or perhaps Barry had questioned his fatherhood, you and I look as much like father and son as you and he do, don't we? —But whatever had happened between them, clearly DNA testing, or any discussion of the paternity issue, was impossible—though, in fact, I did once begin to broach the topic, cautiously, when Barry and I were having lunch together—he flinched, and was even quite cold with me for a while after that. Why did *I* want to know? Perhaps it was advancing age, the prospect of a lonely death and so on, and after losing Piet, seeing him die slowly and painfully. So—were *you* a reason why I came back? I don't think I thought that at the time, but now—I wonder. —When I would see you, when you served me in the Library or I would see you walking there and back, I longed to talk to you, to be in touch, to help you, to be your friend, to be your Father—it was unbearable sometimes—I longed so much to talk to you—I remember once you were serving me at the main desk in the Library and I nearly broke down in the effort to keep self-control—I thought you might notice—and you looked and especially sounded so like him when I first met him—it was torture, I couldn't show my feelings, I couldn't say anything at all, to you or anyone else, it was truly torture. And now I'm—I can't stop, I'm telling you everything. And I hope you see what you've done, *I'm* the one crying now, old fool that I am. Too pitiful to deserve your anger. But look at your situation this way, my dear. You have had *two* Fathers, and most men barely have one. Nature and nurture—you have had a natural Father, the One who started you off with his semen and genes, *and* you have had a nurturing one—your only problem, apart from the fact that one is dead, is to distinguish between the two. But why bother? My advice would be to think of us both, Barry and I, as nurturing—or wanting to be in my case. Does it matter now which one of us was your natural Father?"

I have tried to recall and record as accurately as I can all that Ben said that morning and afternoon, on Christmas Day—though I still feel quite ashamed of my outburst, of 'losing it', screaming, crying. I know the whole episode's of little or no significance for anyone else, anyone who might, sometime in the future, if there is one, come upon these four notebooks and skim through their contents. But for me—over the last few days, I have thought hard about all Ben's words, and Dad's words, all the fragments of their lives which also partly define my life, its origin, its evolution, its actuality—right up to where I am now. And then what? Ben believes that there are many more of us human beings, even millions more of us, surviving around the world, and that human and animal life will continue, though with major changes, some of which he says will be unpredictable but positive, once the Brown Death has run its course—the population will be much smaller of course, but that will be positive too, he says—"just think of how small the population of England was when Shakespeare wrote his plays!" I tell him he's an optimist, and that I think it's almost if not completely over, human existence, civilization, technology, the great silenced cities filled with useless marvels—and he smiles calmly and tells me I'm a pessimist. Will we know who is right? I doubt it. I guess I hope *he* is, but when I think of what we know at this point, little as it is, and when I look out over the dry brown landscape and reluctantly breathe the brown odorous air—well, I find it impossible to be optimistic. Still—I am alive and I have Ben, I have a friend who is also my Father—maybe for not much longer, so all the more to be enjoyed, appreciated.

Since our conflict and reconciliation, we have both been quiet, apart from the short aftermath of Mr Death's death—Ben has been mostly listening to his music, his CDs, "God's second great kindness to me," he says, "the Berlioz *Requiem* is Heaven on Earth, it is the most glorious music I have ever heard, I'd like to die with it in my ears and my heart, 'Sanctus, sanctus, sanctus'"— And meanwhile, apart from daily housework in Ben's house, I have been working in the Library mostly, trying to complete the re-shelving, and tidying files and even dusting furniture and computer-screens, and so on. I spent the night of Christmas Day in our house, I think I wrote that earlier—that was partly at Ben's suggestion, no doubt to help repair our relations. "I'd love to have you with me again tonight, my dear, I've never slept so well in my life as last night, but I think perhaps you should be with your parents for at least one night more, and sleep in your own bed, I know I would want that—" and I silently completed his sentence "—before we leave," for I was sure that was in his mind. A day later, he remarked, "Whatever happens, my dear, I really don't relish dying here, like a rat in a cellar"—he was back in the basement then, after telling me the day after Christmas that he wanted to go back down, even though it was colder and a bit smellier there—he said that his feet and hands were perceptibly getting very numb, number and tremblier, and that, when I hadn't been there to help him, during Christmas Night, he had had a hard and painful struggle to reach the bathroom and then get back to his bed—it was much easier for him to cope in the basement, and sleep in the armchair. But it couldn't continue anyway, the way we were living, I knew that—and knew that I was approaching the moment when I'd have to take the decision I'd been dreading. After the one night of sleeping in my bed at home, I slept for three nights again on the couch in Dad's Office in the Library, walking across to Ben's house to have meals and spend a short time with him each morning and afternoon. I guess I was trying to keep some distance between us, maybe there was still a sliver of anger or resentment in me, and some shame over my outburst, or maybe I was merely trying to avoid the moment of decision, but it was also more than that—I should admit here that—in spite of myself, maybe—I was enjoying the feeling of power over Ben—I who had lived in quiet subservience for so many years, I was suddenly in charge, I was master of the situation.

On the third day after Christmas, Ben had said suddenly, "I want to apologize, my dear, for not being at Barry's funeral. I loved him more than you or anyone else could fully understand, and when he had his second heart attack and then was in hospital again, I did want so much, so very much, to be with him, but I had to consider Julie's wishes—I called her as soon as I heard, one of my colleagues informed me, that he had died— those were the days just before the University officially closed down, you remember, when I and some others were still lecturing, and supervising graduate students, I was still going in to my office in the English Department then—but after I had tried to tell her over the phone how sorry I was, how devastated I felt for her and myself, I could judge from her tone, polite and cool and impersonal, that I was right, she hadn't wanted me there, in the hospital, and didn't want me at the funeral—and that was also the last time I spoke over the phone, the line was dead after that. But I should have put my love for Barry first, and his for me. I shouldn't have let her control me—have so much power over me. And after that there was *her* death—I saw you bringing her home after Barry's funeral, and then there was silence for a while, must have been about a week, until I heard a noise in your yard, and went up the stairs to investigate and stood looking out through the window in the side door, where you saw me later, that night before Christmas—and I saw you digging her grave and then carrying her body out the back door into the yard, and I couldn't watch any more, it was too painful, like some nightmare—I came straight back down here to the basement, and went on writing my book. But now I think I should have joined you, we should have buried her together, that would have been my tribute to her and Barry— whatever happened between us later, she gave a young graduate student so much kindness. I owe them both an apology, and you too." I said nothing, judging what he said to be possibly tactical as well as surely truthful. And what was there to say?

On one of my evening walks from Ben's house to the Library, I thought I saw movements in the near-distance— coyotes? but it was too dark for me to be sure, and I wondered if my eyes were deceiving me. Before I went to the Office, and Dad's couch, to sleep that night, I made my way up to the roof, for the second time—with the flashlight, and wearing a face- mask, as I always do now, when I go outside. Up there—it was almost dark—I turned off the flashlight and walked round the circumference, looking down on all four sides of the building, but couldn't see any movement at all. However, later that night I woke up with my heart beating fast and unevenly, and I was panting, my body trembling and sweaty—and I realized after moments of terror that I was in the middle of a nightmare—I had been watching a ring of coyotes closing on the Library, snuffling menacingly, fangs flashing, jaws slavering—and advancing nearer and nearer, out of the darkness, until their snarling faces loomed right at the front door, spattering it with their spittle, and that's when I woke up. —The message seemed clear—I must defend the Library against all its enemies, and at all costs! As I settled myself again, shakily, for sleep, I decided that the time for decision had arrived—tomorrow I must face Ben.

But when I did that, after the three nights of sleeping in the Library and working hard during the days to finish the re-shelving and tidying, I found that the decision had been made long before—or rather, that it wasn't a decision at all, had never been—in fact, it was merely a belated recognition of reality—including the impracticability of what I had considered to be my duty as University Librarian. My dilemma, or what I had been defining as a dilemma, as an agonizing clash between fulfilling that duty and accepting responsibility towards Ben, had never been a choice at all. Human beings matter more than books. They do. However precious the books, each has been created by a human being, for other human beings to read if they wish to. I had failed to understand the obvious. How could I refuse to commit myself to Ben, how could I merely watch him drifting to a slow painful death? —I had seen him swal-lowing four or five pills every day, and there would surely be little or no chance of replenishing his stock of medication here—I had given him the whole collection of Mum and Dad's pills, mainly pain-killers, that I had found in the bathroom at home when I spent the night there, but how long could they last him? Now I asked myself, too, had there ever been any justifiable point in remaining in the Library as its self-appointed guardian? —against what? —and dying in it eventually, as my supply of food and water inevitably came to an end? But at least I will be leaving it as close to maximal functionability as I can. Assuming that humanity survives, here it will stand, this great University Library, holding its vast store of knowledge and wisdom for the hopefully beneficent use of future generations of students. Books may have been challenged and even to some extent displaced during this past decade or so, by the Internet, and ebooks, and so on—but they have survived, they are here, they are beautiful, they are potent, and maybe one day new books will be created and join their elders on the Library's packed shelves, and be read, and valued, and loved. As if to endorse these optimistic thoughts—when I walked towards the Library yesterday afternoon, it looked no longer like a stranded grey whale, slowly expiring, but like a great freighted galleon, an ark, ready to encounter the future, to sail far across the pale brown sea on which, for now, it rests, and waits. And if humanity does *not* survive, then all the knowledge and wisdom the Library has housed, all the literature it has protected, all its myriad books, will be merely a slowly crumbling excrescence, an empty anthill. And the world that surrounds it will probably be inhabited by only insects, animals, birds. —Birds! Birds, birds— How long is it since I heard birdsong, those melodious chants of joy and freedom? —have all birds been asphyxiated by the poisonous brown fog that is now their environment? The memory of birdsong, and a flaring momentary vision of bright wings flickering from tree to fragrant tree—was this an epiphany? —Yes. Yes. And I am filled now with a sudden pain—with a feeling of intense loss. —But soon Ben and I will venture out together, each of us leaving our refuge, moving out into uncertainty, into the future.

This morning I found Ben asleep in his black armchair, his head twisted sideways, his mouth open, just as I had seen him once before, when I'd thought how much he looked like Dad on his deathbed—and for a moment I thought with a start that he was dead too. "Ben," I whispered, touching his prickly chin—for of course we are both of us quite heavily bearded and moustachioed now, having given up trying to shave a while back. His eyes opened and he smiled widely, "My dear, I am so glad to see you. I have been dreaming of Barry and Julie—and you were there too, a small child running about, laughing in the sunlight—though I never saw you at that age. Will you pass me some water, please? My mouth is so dry. And I have a favour to ask." So he too has had an epiphany, I thought. After he had sipped some water, and I had pulled the blanket up to his neck, I sat down opposite him and said "*Another* favour, *another* favour, Dr Bowman? But first, do you know what today is? I hope you do!" "Oh, you won't catch me out so easily, my dear. It is the twenty-ninth of December. And it is your forty-first birthday. What gift can I give you to commemorate so august an occasion?" I was half-surprised, and quite moved. "I don't need anything. Honest, nothing." "Not even my love? Come here, bend down," and when I did, he kissed me lightly on my forehead. "But I do have an announcement to make," I said quickly, standing back. "That we will depart from this place on the first of January, if you are willing to accompany me. Are you?" He smiled again. "Oh my dear, come here for another kiss—and if you want a third—" "No, Ben, two are enough, I'm not Dad!" "Well, you look and sound more and more like him to me—just as beautiful as he was in his prime, when I first met him, that's you, my dear—pity I'm just an old curmudgeon now, nothing to offer at all!" "Well, we must talk about preparations and arrangements. —But what about that favor?" "It's a simple one, and won't take very long." He held out a small book with a black cover, "This is an old copy of the South African Anglican *Book of Common Prayer*—Piet gave it to me when he was dying, it was a gift from his mother when he set off for university—he was very religious then, he had always treasured it— and he said he hoped it would help to bring me to God—well, no, it won't, I'm too much of a sinner for that, but I was very impressed by his deep devotion and firm beliefs—I told you I became a member of the Cathedral congregation here, didn't I? and that was because of him, I'm sure. I know you are an atheist like Barry, or an agnostic, most people are these days, or were— though I noticed that you chose *The Four Quartets* as your favourite poem, and you must know that Eliot was a fervent Christian when he wrote that—and quoted, from the four- teenth-century nun Julian of Norwich, that statement of enraptured optimism, 'All shall be well and all shall be well.' — But I'm saying all this only as a prelude to formally requesting my favour. What I would like, now on your birthday, is for us to read aloud together the Burial Service, as my tribute, our tribute, to Barry and Julie. Yes?" So I helped him up the stairs, and again we sat together, and read aloud alternately from the small book. And I thought also about Elise, and Thumper, and even Mr Death. —Oh Elise, you haven't been in my mind for so long, it's been so crammed with Ben and my past and— Please come back— But my time is growing short, and I won't attempt to quote here from the Burial Service—the *Book of Common Prayer* is with Ben anyway—I'll only say how moving I found the Psalms—23, 90, and 130, "Out of the deep have I called unto thee, O Lord"—and "Man that is born of woman hath but a short time to live, and is full of trouble"—and when Ben pronounced a blessing at the end, one that he remembered from Cathedral communion services and that he said he espe- cially loved, I found myself in tears, "May the Lord make his face to shine upon us, and give us peace."—Shine upon us, oh shine upon us, like the sun that seems to have abandoned us— may it return to us, may it shine upon us, give us health and warmth and life. And peace. Amen, amen, amen.

Moving on is where it's at! Oh, I am into slang clichés today! Another sign, maybe, that I am cheerful, an almost forgotten emotion. Just as Ell's and Ben's incursions into my anxious silence have changed my life forever, impinging on all my thoughts and emotions—so our imminent departure is infusing optimism—the challenge of change, the excited joy of adventure! —I feel a surge not only of optimism, but of renewed vitality. —"We shall not cease from exploration"! I sat down with Ben to plan our departure. There was no need for us to discuss which direction we should go, north, south, east, or west? —It had to be north, along Highway Number Six, for both practical and emotional reasons—one tank of gas would get us to Dad's cottage on the Bruce Peninsula, it certainly wouldn't get us to Ben's brother in British Columbia, if indeed he was still there and alive, and of course there could be no assurance of being able to buy or find gas along the highway— and anyway I knew, and Ben knew, that Dad's cottage would give us assured and familiar shelter, the possibility of starting a new life, and the healing pleasure of being with Dad and Mum in spirit and memory. And after all, our survival to this point is Dad's gift. He bought all the cans of food and soup, and packets of cookies, and plastic bottles of water, that we have been consuming each day—also, as I discovered when I drove Mum to and from his funeral, he had filled the gas tank of his car, the aptly named little green Escape, and had even packed into the back of it further provisions of food and water, as well as most of the camping kit I remember so well from summer holidays during my childhood, including a pup tent, and our small kerosene lamps and cooker, with matches and two cans of kerosene—he had always insisted that the lamps and cooker could be used safely only out-of-doors, we were never allowed to even think of using them in a tent, or indoors—which was obviously why, I informed Ben, only candles had been provided for his house, though I wonder if they are much safer! "There's *my* car as well," Ben said, "but I'm sure that Barry's will be in a far better condition, I know he had it serviced regularly. So that leaves only a supply of suitable clothes and toiletry and towels,

and of reading and writing materials." "I'll see to the former," I
said, "if you will take charge of the latter—I'll pack our suitcases
and load them—but we must be careful not to overload the car,
I don't want to be changing a tire in cold or darkness—actually I
fear I might be too weak to manage that, especially if the air is
even more polluted as we travel north, though I hope it will be
the opposite! —Maybe we'll have to wear our masks all the
way." "Right. I wish I could take my CD player, and CDs, but I
know we won't have space, and anyway the batteries can't last
much longer—so reading and writing will be essential, I'll take
the second copy of my book, you can leave the first copy in the
Library—and when we get to the cottage, I hope you'll at last
read and criticize it, and will you please bring all of your poems
and perhaps some of your short stories? —And after that, well, I
guess we must have the Bible and Shakespeare, it will be fun to
read *The Tempest* together, I will be Caliban and you will be
Ariel and we can take turns being Prospero. —And what else?
Let's each choose one favourite book of the moment, this very
moment. When you help me up to my office this evening just
before we go to bed, I'll choose *my* one. Then we should be well
provided for whatever future God allows."

So—it is the thirty-first of December, we leave tomorrow
morning. "In the end is my beginning." "We shall not cease
from exploration." When I came over to the Library to try to
complete this record, this 'diary without dates'—actually 'diary
with a few dates'—I was wondering which book I would take
with me into the future, and at last opened Bertrand Russell's
History of Western Philosophy, B72.R8—which had been
waiting so patiently on Dad's desk. —Of course I looked first at
what he had to say about our beloved Heraclitus, and was
shocked to read that in Russell's opinion Heraclitus had been
"much addicted to contempt" and "believed in war"—what
would Elise and I have made of such unwelcome judgements

during our discussions?—but surely we would have agreed that Heraclitus "was a mystic." —In fact, I guess they're all mystics, the philosophers and poets whose thoughts about our existence have been preserved—and *we* are mystics too—all of us sinful confused human-beings condemned to the struggle of trying to make sense of a world infinitely too complex for our puny comprehension—fragments, so many fragments—an implacable mass of fragments is all we can achieve. But I'm wasting precious time and effort on these tangential and no doubt repetitive final comments. Am I deliberately procrastinating? I have decided not to take Russell's book with me—for one thing, it's too heavy, physically as well as in its content—but when I went upstairs to replace it, and gaze for the last time at the ranged mass of shelved philosophy books, I suddenly noticed a small red-covered volume, published in 1911, entitled *Comfortable Words for Christ's Lovers, being the Visions and Voices vouchsafed to Lady Julian, recluse at Norwich in 1373,* BV 4831.J82. Extracting this book from among its companions on the shelf, I felt a moment of guilt at taking it out of the Library and into the world, neither signed-out nor likely ever to be returned—but then Elise spoke to me: "Don't be silly, she is the first woman who wrote literature in English, a work of such spiritual profundity that centuries later her influence remains potent and beneficent—I heartily approve of your taking her with you, indeed I guided you to her, she wrote that book for you, and everyone who will ever read her words— words that preserve her fragments of insight into the nature of reality—but remember that, as a medieval Christian, she writes within a context very different in many ways from ours. I am united with her and with you, and with our beloved Heraclitus, we are united, the four of us, in thought, emotion—the four of us are One—'Sin is behovely, but all shall be well and all shall be well, and all manner of thing shall be well.'"

Yes, Elise. I hear you. But Mum and Dad and Ben and me—the four of *us* are also One. My love for them, my gratitude for all they have given me, are just as deep. And perhaps for Dad above all, he gave me the Library as my home—and I could never begin to acknowledge adequately the significance and joy of that gift. But I have learned now to qualify your angry opinion, Dad, that all the changes introduced in this Library after your retirement as University Librarian have been catastrophic. Yes, reading, like writing, is primarily a solitary activity, and may require temporary isolation and silence—I agree, I agree—but appreciation, criticism and learning are essentially social, communal, the fruit of conversation, argument, debate—and surely a Library can and should provide for both? The silence that you idealized in this Library could also be cold, oppressive—I experienced that sometimes, but would not admit it—while the gentle buzz of students studying together in a reading room, using together the gifts of learning and technology, could be warm, welcoming, and clearly creative. Yes, I am changing too, Dad—primarily through the liberating and empowering influence of Elise and Ben. I was immured for too long in silence and isolation—but they broke through those prison walls, Elise and Ben, and freed me—separately and together, they gave me a priceless gift, the healing delight of conversation and friendship. No, I don't think I am betraying you, Dad, though at first I wondered about that, and began to feel guilty— but truly it is positive acceptance of change, not a shift of personal allegiance. I hope you would agree that I have been, briefly and unexpectedly, and quite unofficially, a satisfactory successor of you, and Dr Goode, as University Librarian—doing my best, in my circumstances, to preserve and protect this Library—mine a simple direct responsibility compared to yours, but one I have worked hard to fulfill—so that this Library is ready for any successor of ours, any University Librarian of the future, to control and administer, in the service of its readers and of the accumulated knowledge and wisdom it holds. I hope you would respect what I have done here.

As Heraclitus knew, as all philosophers, as every one of us knows, change is inevitable, an insistent cliché of this fiery world—whether positive or negative in effect, whether a universal social collapse enforced by a huge disaster like AIMD, or our individual responses to everyday situations and relationships as they, too, change. "You cannot step twice into the same river; for fresh waters are always flowing upon you." Yes—that is our essential reality—change and chance—chance that the thoughts of Heraclitus were preserved, chance that I met Elise, chance that Piet died of AIDS and Ben came here— chance, chance. But we define ourselves, our morality, our humanity, through the choices we make as our world spins around us—choosing to treat our fellow humans, and all animals, with love, compassion, respect—and our common inheritance, this prolific world, with restraint and appreciation. Each of us simultaneously an individual and merely another evanescent expression of the herd. We are, and are not. And I guess, in the end, we human beings can only live our hope that even the most painful and destructive changes will, ultimately, be beneficent—that all shall be well, all things shall be well.

What more is there to say? I have written too much already, on these final pages—a veritable peroration, and in a style more verbose and pompous and didactic than Ben's in his memoir, I fear! But in a few minutes I'll be finished, write my final words, and be ready to leave the Library, this afternoon—and my parents' house, and Ben's house, and Westgreen, tomorrow morning. I will place this notebook, with its three companions, in Dad's secret drawer, just below and in front of me as I sit for the last time at his desk in his Office. Then I will leave this

Library, which I have loved and valued and where I have found great happiness and fulfillment. I will close its front door but not lock it. And with Ben, the friend who is my Father, the Father who is my friend, I will fare forward.

Here, now, everywhere, always.
These fragments—
We are, and are not.

ABOUT THE AUTHOR

Peter Abbot lives and writes in Hamilton, Ontario. His is also the author of the novel *Voice of the Lord*, available from Rock's Mills Press.